Praise for
Great Ball of Light

"Eerie and hopeful: family tragedy and reconciliation wrapped in a zombie encounter." —*Kirkus Reviews*

". . . intelligent, wry, and thoughtful." —*Bulletin of the Center for Children's Books*

". . . a fun book for the younger zombie-loving set." —*School Library Journal*

"What would you do if you discovered a ball of light able to resurrect the dead? This faintly macabre story has plenty of humorous moments and will surely leave readers wondering about life and death and the stages in between." —*Booklist*

Also by Evan Kuhlman

Brother from a Box
The Last Invisible Boy

Great Ball of Light

Evan Kuhlman

Evan Kuhlman

illustrated by ~~Jeremy Holmes~~ Fiona North

A
atheneum

A Caitlyn Dlouhy Book

ATHENEUM BOOKS FOR YOUNG READERS
New York   London   Toronto   Sydney   New Delhi

ATHENEUM BOOKS FOR YOUNG READERS

An imprint of Simon & Schuster Children's Publishing Division

1230 Avenue of the Americas, New York, New York 10020

This book is a work of fiction. Any references to historical events, real people, or real places are used fictitiously. Other names, characters, places, and events are products of the author's imagination, and any resemblance to actual events or places or persons, living or dead, is entirely coincidental.

Text copyright © 2015 by Evan Kuhlman

Cover and interior illustrations copyright © 2015 by Jeremy Holmes

All rights reserved, including the right of reproduction in whole or in part in any form.

ATHENEUM BOOKS FOR YOUNG READERS is a registered trademark of Simon & Schuster, Inc.

Atheneum logo is a trademark of Simon & Schuster, Inc.

For information about special discounts for bulk purchases, please contact Simon & Schuster Special Sales at 1-866-506-1949 or business@simonandschuster.com.

The Simon & Schuster Speakers Bureau can bring authors to your live event. For more information or to book an event, contact the Simon & Schuster Speakers Bureau at 1-866-248-3049 or visit our website at www.simonspeakers.com.

Also available in an Atheneum Books for Young Readers hardcover edition

Book design by Debra Sfetsios-Conover

The text for this book was set in Janson Text LT Std.

The illustrations for this book were rendered in charcoal pencil and watercolor.

Manufactured in the United States of America

0116 OFF

First Atheneum Books for Young Readers paperback edition February 2016

10 9 8 7 6 5 4 3 2 1

The Library of Congress has cataloged the hardcover edition as follows:

Kuhlman, Evan.

Great ball of light / Evan Kuhlman. — First edition.

pages cm

Summary: When a ball of light appears with the power to bring the dead back to life, twins Fiona and Fenton are determined to catch it and perform some experiments.

ISBN 978-1-4169-6461-2 (hc)

ISBN 978-1-4169-6462-9 (pbk)

ISBN 978-1-4424-2661-0 (eBook)

[1. Dead—Fiction. 2. Brothers and sisters—Fiction. 3. Twins—Fiction.] I. Title.

PZ7.K9490113Gr 2015

[Fic]—dc23

2013049286

A Handy Guide to
Bringing Back the Dead
(Take 1)

What you will need:

- A wheelbarrow to transport your tools and the zombie you've chosen to awaken in case he can't walk or has no legs (rats might have eaten them).
- Two shovels if there are two of you.
- Two flashlights if you plan to dig at night.
- A tire iron or other tool that can open a sealed casket.
- Gloves so your hands don't get blistered while digging.
- A baseball bat to defend yourself with in case the zombie attacks you.
- Snacks and beverages—you will be digging for a while. Note: it's unlikely that your zombie

will ask for food or water, but be prepared just in case. Second note: if he says he wants to "eat your brains," please see the above baseball bat entry.

- A scarf or a mask to cover your nose and mouth so you will not breathe in the stinky rot of death and decay, the worst odor in the universe.

- Dark clothing and Halloween face paint, or some other way to disguise yourself, in case someone sees you at the cemetery or while traveling to and from there.

- A notebook, a pen, and a camera and spare batteries, so you can document the experiment.

- A cell phone (optional) in case the thing you awaken goes on a rampage and you need help from the US Army.

- A really good story in case someone asks you why you are robbing a grave.

- A second good story in case the zombie you brought back can speak and asks why you woke him up.

- A third good story in case something unexpected happens.

- Clothing and a hat for the zombie in case he is as naked as a skeleton.

- A great ball of light capable of restoring life to dead

stuff. Note: unexpected side effects are possible, so be on guard. Second note: there may only be one light ball in the world, so if it shows up in your yard one day please share it with others.

- And, most importantly, you will need tons of courage and lots of good luck.

Picture This . . .

I t's just past midnight, and my brother, Fenton, and I are pushing a wheelbarrow holding our undead grandfather, who we dug up at a cemetery a mile from our farm. There's one of us on each handle—pushing a sort-of-dead guy is a two-kid job.

We are on a tar and gravel road, so pebbles crunch under the wheelbarrow's wheel—maybe this will help you see it inside your head. We pass by houses and farms, some with unattended cows. Cows at night, with their dark eyes and splotchy designs, look like creatures from another planet.

Fenton and I stop pushing Grandpa Wade so we can rest.

"You're such a girl," my brother says to me. "I could

have gone much farther before resting." But he's shaking blood into his arms just like I'm doing.

"And you're such a donkey butt," I say. I try to make a donkey sound but blow it. Mr. Ed with a bad head cold, let's call it.

Anyway.

It had been cloudy all day, but when I check the sky I see stars glittering above us. We live in a small farm town, so nothing blocks our view of the sky. That night, the night Fenton and I commit grave robbery for the sake of our family, it seems like the stars are packed ten deep per square foot of sky.

Awe-mazing.

"Stars," my grandfather says, pointing at the sky with a crooked finger. He died three years ago in a car wreck, and by all rights he had given up his star-seeing privileges. But a miracle happened, and now he's seeing stars again.

Watching Grandpa watch the stars, it hits me that I should never take anything for granted, like seeing stars fill up the sky on a warm night in May—and a hundred other things and people I love. Because one day it could all be gone, and if I'm waiting on a miracle to bring it back, I might be waiting for a very long time.

me

Introductions

My name is Fiona North and I'm nearly thirteen years old. My brother, Fenton, is the same age. We are twins, the fraternal kind, so we don't much look like each other, except for blue eyes of the exact same shade and earlobes that look a little pulled on.

According to our mom and dad, Fenton was born eleven minutes before I was. I'm still mad at myself for not showing more ambition and being the first one born: What was I waiting for, an invitation? Or, knowing my brother, maybe he pushed me aside so he could be the first one out.

dork bro

We live on a farm in Deerwood, Montana, that I named Bluebird Acres after we moved there from

Great Falls. If you look at a map—a magnifying glass might be helpful—you will find Deerwood down at the bottom, in the center of the state and just east of the Gallatin National Forest.

Deerwood is so small we go to school and shop for groceries in a neighboring town called Red Lodge, which is also small, but big enough to have schools and stores and a gas station and doctors and a place where they hold rodeos during the summer. Sometimes we see a moose roaming around. It's a cool town.

Our dad is named William, but everyone calls him Will, not Bill. He works on our farm and takes handyman jobs to earn extra cash: it's hard to make lots of money selling corn, eggs, and goat milk. Sometimes Fenton and I barely see him except at breakfast, especially if he's going to be on the other side of the county, repairing a fence or patching a roof, or visiting his girlfriend. My brother and I call her the Ice Queen. I'll tell you more about her later on.

Fenton's and my mom is named Amanda Carson, and she lives 2,149.41 miles away in New York City, so we only see her for two weeks each summer and hardly ever talk to her on the phone because she is always busy, busy, busy. If you flip through ladies' magazines at the drugstore with the hope of seeing pictures of women in their underwear—*like Fenton does*—you might know my mom's name since she writes articles for those magazines about fashion and makeup and what celebrities do when they aren't making movies or starring in TV shows.

I think it's strange that my mother, who carried me in her crowded belly for nine months and fed me and taught me some cool stuff before she left Montana, like how to attract hummingbirds to our property (planting trumpet creepers and bee balm did the trick), and who pretty much lived in jeans and T-shirts, would want to have a job writing about dopey stuff like lipstick and fashion labels, but maybe her parents did not raise her right, or something else went wrong along the way.

There are things Mom and I do have in common. We both love books and writing. I have read all the Harry Potter books, the Lord of the Rings trilogy, the Lemony Snicket series, the Hunger Games trilogy, and many more: my bedroom is like a miniature library. And now I'm writing my own book, sorta. Hopefully, I won't totally screw it up, but you can be the judge.

Now, without further delay, I'd like to tell you an incredible story that you might find hard to believe, even though it's true. It begins on the next page. So why are you still on this one?

Stormy Weather

Like most great stories this one starts with a storm, the kind that will curl your hair due to fright and electricity, and make you wish you were living underground with moles as your neighbors, since that's the only safe place when nasty storms strike.

Unless of course they are psycho murderer moles. . . . Anyway.

This particular storm hit at about four thirty that afternoon, a warm day in May. Fenton and I had been home from school for an hour and were watching TV when there was a *beep . . . beep . . . beep*, and then words scrolled across the screen saying that the National Weather Service in Cheyenne had issued a thunderstorm warning for the following counties, and our county, Carbon County, was one of them. We had nine minutes of peace to enjoy before the thunderstorm attacked our farm, said the scroll.

This storm is capable of producing heavy rain, hail, damaging winds, and possible tornadoes. Those within the path of the storm should take cover immediately.

"And kiss your stinky butts good-bye," said Fenton, adding words that were not on the screen. I tried to smile, but it wasn't working. Ever since I was a baby I've been terrified of storms. Back then, according to my mother, I would cry and shake whenever thunder boomed and lightning flashed.

I'm over the crying part, but I'm still frightened of storms. My fear is not something I would admit to Fenton, however. He is brave and often reckless, and I want to be brave too, and slightly less reckless.

Before we could look outside and check on the storm, the phone in the kitchen rang. Fenton was closest, so it was his job to answer it. He stood up and I did too. I followed him into the kitchen, and then huddled close so I could hear our father say over the phone that a bad thunderstorm was coming, so we should go into the storm cellar until it cleared. He also said that he was doing some indoor electrical work and it was going slower than he had planned, so we should have dinner without him.

"Love you guys," he said. Fenton and I told our father we loved him, too, then Fenton hung up. I wished I had told Dad that he should take a break from working and hide from the storm. Sometimes parents issue advice to their kids that they do not heed themselves, such as to not stay up too late or you'll be grumpy the next morning and your hair will be weird and you will hiss at singing birds and tell them to shut their tiny traps if they know what's good for them.

Fenton turned off the TV, then we went outside, stood on the porch, and looked west, to see what the storm was doing. It seemed like we were looking at every kind of cloud God had ever invented. There were tall clouds and flat ones and thick ones and wispy ones. Some were smooth, others had ruffles and layers. Cirrus clouds and stratus clouds and other kinds of clouds with names I couldn't remember. There were white clouds and gray ones and purple ones and blue ones, and some black clouds were scooting lower than the other clouds like they didn't want to be seen with them.

"Do you think we'll see a twister today?" I asked Fenton, the self-proclaimed expert on all matters of the world—surely he would have an opinion.

"I sure hope so." He looked at the clouds like he was trying to will them into forming a funnel cloud, that twisting finger of doom.

"Me too," I agreed, trying to sound tough as nails, though I didn't really want to see a tornado, not that day, not ever. Anything that kills people and animals and wrecks their homes is no friend of mine, no matter how cool they look on TV.

We heard a goat bleating out back and remembered our father's other instruction, to make sure the animals were in the barn or their coop. Our animal inventory that day included three goats, eleven chickens, two ducks, and two cats. One thing I've learned about farm animals is that they have a better sense that a storm is coming than most people. So we didn't have much work to do. Daisy the one-eared goat needed to be pushed and spooked and encouraged to go inside the barn, but all the other animals, except the cats, were sheltered. We figured that Piedmont (orange) and Screech (black) had enough sense to find their own shelter when the rain started. Sure enough, when thunder boomed far off, Piedmont scrambled down from the highest branch of the old dead maple tree out front, his favorite perch, and tore off for safer quarters.

Fenton and I peered again at the sky. Storm clouds,

all of them looking darker and meaner than they had three minutes ago, seemed to be racing to see which one could get to us first. There was a flash of lightning in the distance, and thunder growled and tried to scare us. We could see sheets of rain falling three farms over, though our property was still dry. But the wind was crazy, coming from every direction and tugging at our clothes like it was rudely trying to turn us into naked people.

"Time to go in the storm cellar," I said, grabbing Fenton's arm.

He jerked away. "We have another minute or two. Don't be such a big baby."

Another streak of lightning cut through the sky. I glared at Fenton. Everyone with a working brain knows that just because lightning from an approaching storm isn't directly above you, that does not mean you are safe.

Before I could spit out any choice words, Mother Nature put on a demonstration as to why Fenton's assumption of safety was dead wrong. A third lightning bolt shot out of the sky. This one blasted into the lawn about twenty feet in front of us, not far from the dead maple tree, briefly setting a patch of grass on fire and causing every hair I owned to shoot straight out.

Immediately thunder sonic-boomed, knocking us on our butts. I had never heard of lightning striking the ground, or thunder knocking down kids. Things were not adding up right in my head. Two plus two equals frog.

"Did you see the lightning strike the lawn?" Fenton cried out as we clambered to our feet and slapped our ears. Mine were pounding but seemed to hear okay.

"I saw it, heard it, and felt it," I said. "We could have been killed. Storm cellar. Now!"

Even though I'm eleven minutes younger than Fenton, on the rare occasions when I use my I'm-in-charge-and-I-know-what's-best voice he'll normally go along with my wishes. And so he did that day, briefly.

We were scooting to the storm cellar, wind cutting at us and electricity charging up the air, when my brother looked back at where the lightning bolt had struck the grass and said, "Hey, Fiona, look at what the lightning did!"

That was when I split myself in two, amoeba style. (A process called *binary fission*, in case you haven't been paying attention in science class.)

Part of me, including some of my best elements like smartness and common sense and the will toward self-preservation, urged me to keep going to the storm cellar, to not even look back for a quick second to see what Fenton was talking about.

But I'm also made up of elements such as curiosity, and I have learned that curiosity owns a big roll of duct tape and likes to tape over the mouths of those other, more sensible voices, leaving it the loudest.

So I stopped and looked back, and saw something bizarre: the lightning had cut a crater into the yard, about a foot wide. Steam rose out of it. It was creepy looking, like the earth had been gashed and was leaking steam.

Cautious

duct tape

My first thought was that I had seen this movie before. The movie where lightning or a space ray blasts a hole in the ground, and then two kids of questionable brain wattage step closer to the hole to investigate, and as soon as they stick their heads above the crater—*slurp!*—an alien monster pulls them into its huge mouth and gobbles them up in three bites.

"Fenton! Storm cellar!" I cried.

Besides the threat of being eaten by an alien monster, the storm was nearly on top of us. Pinging drops of rain from the nearing sheets were hurling themselves at us, a warning that zillions of their friends were on the way.

"Hang on a sec, Fi," he said. "I have to see what's down there." Sometimes Fenton gets a look on his face that is part sinister, part curiosity, and part thrill from doing something dangerous. That triple combo was in play at that moment, and I knew, as I always did in those situations, that nothing I said or did would stop him from looking into the hole in our lawn, alien monsters be darned.

Fenton inched closer to the steaming crater, ignoring the thickening rain and thunder booms.

My brain was screaming: run to the cellar, open the doors, and hide; save yourself from the thunderstorm and whatever was inside the crater (my logical self had sent the alien monster packing). But the non-screaming-brain part of me didn't want to leave Fenton alone outside to face hazards from the storm. He was my brother and my twin, and in the end I couldn't talk myself into saving my skin and abandoning him.

So I caught up to Fenton. By then the storm was at

full power; rain plastered my clothes to my body and fogged up my eyes.

As we approached the crater I heard a hissing sound and scientifically guessed that it was caused by hot steam rising from the hole in the ground running into cooler raindrops, an unhappy chemical collision, and so the hissing.

"Let's go to the storm cellar like Dad told us to do," I said, a waste of words since there would be no corralling Fenton before he had a chance to see into the crater. I imagined how our father would react when he got the news that his kids had been killed by a lightning storm. It would ruin him. He loved us a lot.

One thing I've learned from my many escapades with Fenton is that with every daring adventure there is a point of no return, and the point is not always where you think it should be. Like the time Fenton talked me into leaping from the barn loft and onto some hay bales. The point of no return was not when I jumped from the loft, but when I left Fenton's side and stepped closer to the edge so I could scope out how far the drop was and guess at the likelihood of serious injury or death. By even considering the jump and the logistics to survive it, the die had been cast. It was just a matter of when I would leap, how loud

I would scream, and if my life would flash before my eyes as I fell.

On the day of the storm I think the point of no return was when Fenton and I got within two feet of the steaming crater, close enough that a monster arm (I was reconsidering that possibility) could fling out of the fissure and wrap us up in its slimy grip and crush us before we could call for help. And close enough that curiosity was in charge, the last squeal of good sense having been silenced a minute earlier.

And close enough that we could peer inside the crater. As we were about to do that, something amazing happened: a ball of light shot out of the hole and began to bounce around the yard. Its size was between a cantaloupe and a kickball. I had never seen anything like it before.

"What is that?" Fenton asked, like I was some kind of expert on light balls, or bizarre phenomena in general.

"I don't know, but don't get near it—we could get burned. Come on, it's time to go into the cellar." I figured that if the lightning bolt created the light ball, it must be at least a thousand degrees Fahrenheit. (I later learned that the air around a lightning bolt could get as hot as fifty thousand degrees.)

For about a minute, as rain pelted us and lightning prongs lit up the dark sky, my brother and I watched the lightning ball hop around the yard in an unsettled kind of way, like it was unsure what it was doing here or where it should go. I wondered if it was trying to find the crater so it could hide itself underground.

It was then that my brother announced his craziest idea to date, and believe me there have been many crazy ideas—a disastrous indoor fireworks show comes to mind. The idea: we would catch the ball of light, trap it in something, so it could not return to the sky or the crater, or wherever it was planning to go.

"Have you blown a circuit?" I said as thunder roared to the east of us, the storm rolling along. "It will burn us up! No way should we try to catch that thing." Even though I said "we," I knew that I would be the fool running around the yard trying to catch a lightning ball.

"Come on, Fi," he pleaded. "We might never get this chance again. Plus, if we don't trap it, no one will believe us when we tell them that a lightning ball was rolling around our yard. We've gotta catch it while there's still time."

I glared at my sopping-wet brother. His look said to me *Yes, I am dangerously insane, but you kind of like that I'm insane, and you are going to go along with my latest crazy plan, if for no other reason than this: if you made a list of one hundred fun things to do, none of them would come close to catching a lightning ball and keeping it around for everyone to see. Heck, we might even get our picture in the weekly newspaper out of Red Lodge, the* Carbon County News.

It's not with pride that I admit this, but I almost always go along with Fenton's risky ideas and adventures. I think part of it comes from wanting to avoid conflict (and a bruising arm punch) by refusing to cooperate, and another part of it comes from wanting to be a good sister and a friend to Fenton, not one of those dopey girls who would never consider doing anything that could lead to a broken fingernail or a mussed hairdo.

But the biggest reason I don't usually challenge my brother after he's announced his latest insane plan is because the kid knows how to have fun. Yes, it's usually the dangerous kind of fun, but that's okay, since danger makes the adventure something worth remembering. *The day I survived riding a goat while both of us were blindfolded.* That kind of fun.

As rain beat down relentlessly, I thought about what I could use to catch a lightning ball. I nixed a cardboard box or anything made out of plastic—the ball would melt it or burn through it. Then I remembered the glass barrel jar that Dad used to make sun tea. I ran to the porch, grabbed the jar, twisted off the lid, dumped the tea, and ran back to the front yard.

The light ball was hurling itself into the air and bouncing down again. No way would it fit inside the barrel jar. Kickball-sized light ball, softball-sized opening—you do the math. But at least I could tell Fenton that I had tried to catch it.

"Fiona! Hurry up!" he urged. "Before it gets away!"

Before it gets away? The lightning ball, or whatever it was, didn't seem to be in any hurry to leave our property and return to the sky, or wherever lightning balls usually went; it kept bouncing and rolling like it was being swatted by a huge invisible cat.

I gave Fenton an evil-eye death stare, then I stepped cautiously toward the ball of light, holding the barrel jar in front of me like I was hoping it would play nice and leap inside. Trembling and soaked and thinking *I'm too young to die*, I was sure Fenton was getting a kick out of the whole thing.

For a minute or two the lightning ball and I played a game where as soon as I got close it would hop away, and I'd chase it, and then it would tease me like it was ready to cooperate, only to bounce away again. How fun! I was about to order the light ball to go inside the jar *or else*, when it suddenly zinged toward the dead maple tree. It passed through the trunk and came out the other side, none the worse for wear.

Huh—that was weird. It went right through solid wood! But then something even weirder happened. Bright green buds, hundreds of them, began shooting out of the rotten branches of the dead tree. And then the buds popped open and became full-sized maple leaves. It was like a time-lapse movie, except it was real life and real time. From nothing to a tree full of leaves in thirty seconds.

"Whoa!" Fenton said, gawking at the tree.

I couldn't even respond. I was seeing something that was impossible: green life growing out of death.

Fenton snapped out of his awestruck state before I did. "Fiona, we *have* to catch the lightning ball. Look at what it just did!" The maple tree had been dead two minutes earlier, and now it was happy with life. For some reason I wanted to hug the tree and welcome it back to the world.

Anyway.

I was about to suggest that Fenton take a turn trying to catch the light ball, when we caught a break.

The ball bounced toward me in wide arcs, landed on the jar opening, and squeezed itself inside. What? I waited for my hands to catch fire and burn up due to lightning heat, but they didn't. So I did the only rational thing one could do under the circumstances, I twisted on the lid. When my hands *still* didn't burn off, I calmed down enough to realize that the glass was not warm, even though a *lightning ball* was inside it. My next realization was that the ball had a beat to it, like it was alive.

I held the jar as far away from my body as I could, and Fenton and I gaped at it. My brother started to say something, then gave up. I tried to say something deep and meaningful, but my tongue wasn't working right. Fenton and I then shared a look that could be interpreted this way: Now that we actually trapped the freaky thing, what are we supposed to do with it?

We were so caught up gazing at the light ball and giving each other baffled looks, we didn't immediately notice that a rusty red pickup truck was coming up the road at the speed of stupid. It was Sonny Baskins, our next-door neighbor to the west of us, who we hardly knew since he was old and grumpy and would barely wave if we were outside at the same time. Something told me that it wouldn't be a good idea for Sonny to see the ball of light, so I turned away from the road and went inside the house, Fenton right behind me.

Before closing the door, I took one more look at the maple tree—the rain was easing up so I had a pretty good view. The new leaves were still attached to the branches, and there were more of them now. *Wow*, I thought. *Just wow*.

"Go, miracle tree!" I then said, unaware that the rebirth of a dead maple tree was only the first of many miracles yet to come.

Second-Chance Beetles

Not wanting to catch a cold or drip rainwater throughout the entire house, I set the barrel jar on the kitchen table, then I went into my room to dry off and change my clothes. When I returned, the table was empty. For a nanosecond I thought maybe I'd lost my mind—had there really *been* a light ball? Had I imagined the whole thing?

But then a smarter thought crept in: Fenton had taken the jar.

And he had, to his room. It was sitting on his dresser while Fenton examined his collection of dead bugs and small animals (mice and toads) that he kept in the top drawer. My brother was fascinated by what made things tick, and would cut up dead creatures he found on the farm, scooping out their guts and snipping off wings, legs, and feelers. I'd decided this means that one day he will be a skilled surgeon, a dedicated veterinarian, or a famous serial killer.

"What do you think you are doing?" I asked, fearful that I already knew the answer. *Oh no. . . .*

"It's time for some scientific experimentation," he said, extracting a dead beetle from the drawer. It was an inch long and nasty looking.

He examined the bug—it was missing a leg. "I've been thinking," Fenton said slowly, as if he were thinking at that very moment, while he was talking. "If the lightning ball could bring a dead tree back to life, what could it do for a dead beetle or a dead toad? Or a dead anything?"

Before I could stop him, he opened the jar and dropped the bug inside, quickly resealing the lid to keep the light ball from escaping.

I couldn't help myself—I came closer, like my brother, practically pressing my nose against the jar.

The instant miracle we were expecting, a beetle resurrection, didn't happen. It just lay there dead on the bottom of the jar.

"Crud!" Fenton complained. He rubbed his chin and seemed to be thinking—there was a definite burning smell as his brain heated up. "Maybe the beetle is too dead to fix. Let's try something else."

There are degrees of deadness?

Fenton was now pulling a cricket from his collection of dead things—apparently the bug had only died the day before. He dropped it into the jar. We watched, hoping to see the cricket's legs twitch, a clue that the light ball was not a one-hit wonder. But nothing happened—the cricket stayed dead.

My brother was getting frustrated.

"Come on, lightning ball," he said. "You can do it! Make those bugs alive again." He scowled at the light ball and went back to his drawer. He was holding up a dead field mouse that had been stripped of its internal organs, when I saw something unbelievable.

"Look . . . Look! Look at the beetle!" I said with spazzy excitement.

"I am," my brother said droopily. "Still dead!"

"No, look closer."

Fenton gazed at the beetle, and his jaw fell open. "Its missing leg—it grew back! Double whoa!"

And, right before our eyes, the beetle began to shake. And then so did the cricket. As for the great ball of light, it throbbed and pulsed as if it were pretty proud of itself.

"This is so incredible," I said, watching the zapped-back-to-life bugs and feeling kind of dreamy—I guess that's the right word—like reality was suddenly whatever Fenton and I wanted it to be.

But my feelings of excitement started to get mixed with something else. . . . What was going on here? Insects did not regrow legs, not that I knew of—not like this. And dead trees didn't suddenly spurt out green leaves. A huge well of dread started filling up my stomach.

As I conjured up a biblical-style warning about plagues of locusts descending on us if we did not free the lightning ball and stop all experimentation, Fenton twisted the lid off the jar, scooped up the reanimated bugs, dropped them into his drawer, and resealed the lid.

"We need to treat this like a true scientific experiment," he said, oblivious to everything else, apparently. He looked at me and frowned. "What's with you, Fi? This is AMAZING! Come on! Let's observe these critters and see how long they live. Take notes. And some pictures! So no one can ever doubt us."

"No one who?" I said, refocusing. "What are you talking about?"

"When we go public with our research," he said,

picking up the undead cricket and examining it. "Don't you see what is happening? This is all . . . historic, something that has never happened before! We are going to be rich and famous. Zillionaires! We have the power to bring dead things back to life. People have been dreaming of doing this kind of thing, well, since forever."

I had a sudden vision that my brother had transformed into Dr. Fenton Frankenstein—all that was missing was a lab coat and some funky machinery. I guess that made me his hunchbacked faithful assistant, Igorella.

"*We* are not doing anything," I said. "It's the light ball. . . . It's . . . it's causing the miracles, not us. We're just two dumb kids who happened to catch it."

"Make that two dumb kids who own a lightning ball that can bring back the dead," he said. "Man oh man, just imagine what's going to happen to us. We'll be guests on TV shows like *Montana Morning with Bryce and Ellen*, and we'll be on magazine covers all over the world! Everyone will know our names."

"But we hate that *Montana Morning* show," I pointed out. "Remember how we decided that Bryce was really a robot, and that Ellen—"

"You're missing my point," Fenton interrupted.

"We are going to be rich and famous, and the whole world will be ours!"

I heard him babbling on about the wonders of fame and fortune, but a new thought was overwhelming me. If this thing could bring bugs and trees back to life, what else could it do? What if it could—

"Fiona!" my brother snapped. "Gimme a hand here!"

Okay, focus, I told myself. Focusing will keep my brain from going into scary places. "What do you need?" I asked.

Fenton told me to go get a notebook so *we* could document our scientific experiments. Of course I knew that *I* would be the one doing the work, such as note-taking and observations and compiling photo-graphic evidence, while my brother had all the fun, drop-ping dead things into the jar and watching their little motors kick in.

I was about to fetch a note-book and Dad's camera when the cricket leaped out of Fenton's hand and landed on the rug. I shrieked, even though it was just a cricket. Like how it went in the Frankenstein movies, our little monster was on the loose.

Then it leaped again. But not a *cricket* kind of leap.

I've seen crickets jump eight or ten inches before, but this one was leaping four, even five feet. We hurried over to it—as soon as we got close, it jumped again. Now it was nearly across the room.

"We have to catch it," Fenton said urgently, "so Dad doesn't find it and blast it with Raid."

"I'm trying!" I said, snatching at the cricket but missing. Fenton slammed the door shut so the cricket wouldn't get into the hall.

After several more minutes of mayhem I had a fresh idea. I opened Fenton's window, then stomped near the cricket as it rested on the rug. The undead insect flew out of the opening and landed on some grass.

"Have a happy life," I said as it hopped away in gigantic hops. But then a doomsday image scuttled through my head where the escaped cricket mated with another cricket, and their babies, because their father was filled with lightning, could never die. And the crickets would grow bigger and bigger, and would take over the world and eat people. And Fenton and I would be famous, but for a bad reason: we'd be the kids who ended life as we know it. And we wouldn't be invited to appear on *Montana Morning with Bryce and Ellen*, because Bryce and Ellen will have been *eaten by giant crickets*.

Hoo boy. Poor Bryce and Ellen.

Chapter 5

Life Is a Grilled Cheese Sandwich

Fenton had just dropped a wrinkled worm into the barrel jar when the phone rang, so I ran to answer it. No, it wasn't God saying what do you two knuckleheads think you are doing, messing with the natural order that I worked so hard to establish? Which was good, because how do you even talk to God and not totally freak out?

It was Dad, calling to make sure Fenton and I had made it through the storm okay, and that there wasn't any damage to the farm.

"Everything is cool," I said. "Oh, one tiny thing. The maple tree out front got struck by lightning."

"Really? Oh well, it was dead anyway," he said. "No harm, no foul."

"No harm, no foul," I repeated. For some reason I

could not tell my dad about the ball of light, and how it had brought the dead tree back to life, not to mention some bugs. The words were lined up in my head, and they did not seem believable. It's strange when the truth sounds like a lie.

Dad said he was going to head over to his girlfriend Beverly's house, and he'd be home around eleven, so Fenton and I should send ourselves to bed by ten since it was a school night.

"Cool," I said, though in no way was it cool. But by then Fenton and I were used to our father spending lots of time at the Ice Queen's house, which we did not approve of, since we hated her with all of our hating muscles, mostly because she was not our real mom.

"My love to you and Fenton," Dad said. "And remember to eat at least one vegetable for dinner. And no, sweet pea, donuts do not count as a vegetable."

"Love you, Dad," I said before hanging up. And then I wondered if Dad would love Fenton and me as much when he found out that we had become mad scientists.

I fixed grilled cheese sandwiches for dinner, which was our usual meal when no one was cooking for us. One sandwich for me, and two with extra cheese for

Fenton. I tell you, that kid is nearly all stomach.

We sat at the dining table. There was a lot on my mind.

"I think we should stop the experiments before we do something we'll regret," I said with cheese-bolstered confidence. "Sure, we had some fun, did a few crazy things, but now it's time to free the light ball and move on."

My brother just looked at me, chewing his sandwich.

"What if God gets mad at us for what we've been doing?" I said, firing more ammo. "Or Mother Nature could be totally upset, seeing as how we stole one of her lightning balls and haven't given it back yet. Trust me, we do *not* want God and Mother Nature mad at us."

Fenton wiped his mouth with a napkin but didn't say anything, which caused me to wonder if he was using psychology against me. I was a little too desperate, and he was a little too calm. In that matchup, who had more power?

"Plus," I said, "we are doing things that no kid should be doing. Who are we to bring dead stuff back to life? We need to quit."

Fenton, to my surprise, smiled and said, "Okay. We'll let the lightning ball go."

"Really? Or are you just messing with me?"

"Not at all. You're the smart one, not me. If you think we should stop experimenting, then that's what we will do."

I was getting my way far too easily. Something wasn't right.

"Thanks, Fenton," I said, tense in my stomach and hands. "If you want to do a few more bug experiments before we ditch the light ball, go right ahead."

He finished his sandwich half before answering. "No, that's okay. Let's release the ball after dinner. No need to bring back any more dead beetles or crickets." (Insert meaningful hesitation.) "Of course . . . No, I better not say it. . . . You might get mad."

My brother had already won and I didn't know it. "Say what?" I said, taking the bait but not yet feeling the hook.

"Well," he said, precariously leaning back in his chair. "I was going to say that we only brought back stupid stuff, a few bugs and a worm and a dead tree. It's not like we love any of that stuff, right? Who loves crickets, other than snakes?"

"I'm lost. What exactly are you saying?"

Fenton grinned, and that was when I felt the hook going in. "Say that next month or next year we lose someone we love, like Dad or Grams or Uncle Jack.

We'll probably wish we still had the lightning ball so we could bring them back to life. But no, you are right, Fiona, we should get rid of the most amazing discovery in the entire history of the world. We sure don't want to upset Mother Nature."

I, Fiona the fish, flopped around for a minute, and then I died and was turned into breaded fish sticks.

Errrhhh! "Okay, fine. Fine! We'll keep it, for now. But here's a rule we cannot break: we have to agree on what we want to resurrect. Oh, and this too: no killing something that's alive just to see if we can bring it back to life. The thing has to already be dead before we even consider experimenting on it."

Fenton nodded and we shook hands, sealing our fates. Then he belched, which was his way of celebrating his victory over me in the battle of brain cells. Sigh.

Chapter 6

You Can't Build a Pig from a Slice of Salami

Fenton had taken a salami slice into his room so he could feed the undead insects, which now numbered five, when an idea struck him. He opened the jar lid and dropped the salami inside, close to the pulsing light ball.

"Do your magic," he encouraged the light.

"What magic?" I asked. "What exactly are you hoping for?"

"That the light transforms the pork in the salami into a living pig," he said.

It seemed to be asking a lot of the light ball, and there were some practical considerations, like if the salami slice morphed into a pig there would not be enough room in the jar and it would explode, and there'd be glass flying all over the place. But I kept my mouth shut. And, being a loyal assistant to a madman, I had my pen on standby, ready to write down observations of the next miracle: from cold cut to undead pig!

But nothing happened after two minutes, or five minutes, or ten. No pig snout emerged from the salami slice. No hooves, either. Not even a twisty tail. It was like the light ball was confused, unsure what to do with the mix of meats and fillers and whatever else they throw into that stuff.

So we gave up, richer from the knowledge that the light ball had its limits. Fenton pulled the salami slice from the jar, broke off pieces for the bugs, and ate the rest of it. And I wrote in my science notebook the results of the experiment:

Salami—>pig = massive fail

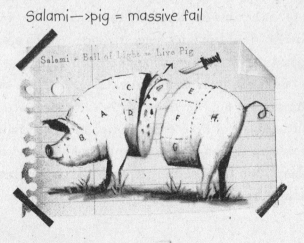

Chapter 7

The Legend of Scruffy the Dog

The next resurrection I blame totally on Nickelodeon.

This was how it started. I coaxed Fenton away from the jar by heating up cherry snack pies in the microwave and declaring a pie-and-TV break. A few minutes later we were watching that cartoon on Nick about a dog that becomes a secret agent, when we had a moment that sometimes happens with twins where we thought the exact same thought.

"Scruffy!" we said. Scruffy was the most loving, big-hearted dog I have ever known, and I've known several great dogs, plus one loser (I'm talking to you, Chester). But because Scruffy was packed with so much love, there wasn't much room left for smarts.

One day last sum-
mer he was chasing the
postal truck like he often
did. But when the truck
stopped so the delivery
lady could stuff mail
into the neighbor's box,
Scruffy, that dumb mutt,
kept going and smashed

into the truck and died instantly. The
mail lady felt bad about it, but it wasn't her fault.

Scruffy was the only dog Fenton and I had owned
since we moved from our house in Great Falls to
the farm in Deerwood. That was a few months
after Grandpa Wade (Dad's dad) died, and his wife,
Grandma Jean, decided she was done with farm life
and moved to an apartment complex in Red Lodge
that only rented to old people.

Back then we were a whole family, though Mom
and Dad had been fighting for a while. When Grandpa
Wade died in a car crash, Dad decided we should
move to the farm where he had grown up. He thought
it would be good for Fenton and me to live in the
country and have animals to care for. We didn't need
much persuading since we loved animals, and while

Great Falls was an okay place to live, it was not such an amazing city that we'd miss it much when we were gone.

Come moving day, after Dad and Fenton and I crawled into the cab of the rental truck, destination Deerwood, and Mom was following us in her car, I kept checking the mirror, certain that the next time I looked my mom would be gone, that she would have taken a right turn or a left turn and we might never see her again. Dad, Fenton, and I were moving to paradise, while Mom was certain she was moving to hell.

Mom followed us all the way there, a trip that lasted nearly five hours since there wasn't a direct route by highway. I think that took a great act of courage on my mother's part, to ignore all those left and right turns and keep driving to Deerwood.

The sad thing is my dad truly believed that Mom would come to love farm life, and that their marriage would be saved since they were doing something they loved, farming, instead of how it was in Great Falls where they had jobs they didn't like much. (Mom managed a beauty shop, and Dad was the chief mechanic at a muffler joint.)

Mom hated farm life, though she only gave it a three-week trial. Then one night in August after a fight with Dad that had something to do with money, Mom said she was running to the store for milk and bread and would be back in a "jiffy." She didn't tell us that the store she was going to was in New York City. Hello, new life. Good-bye, husband and kids and farm poopy smells.

A week after Mom ran away, Dad found Scruffy in the ditch out front; his owner had dropped him off at our farm, which happened a lot, though mostly with unwanted cats. Dad gave the dog to Fenton and me so we would have an animal to love. Not a replacement for our runaway mom, but I understood what he was thinking, that we could benefit from having an affectionate animal friend.

Scruffy was what my dad called a "composite dog," which meant he was several kinds of dog blended into one. Beagle and terrier were some of the parts, but there were many more. In my mind Scruffy got the best of each breed, except for smarts, which I already said. But he was loving and playful, the kind of dog that was at his best when he was with people.

Well, except for the mail-truck thing.

As much as I missed Scruffy, I quickly retreated from the resurrection idea I had shared with Fenton. It was too late to even consider trying to bring back

Scruffy—there'd be almost nothing left of him, nine months after his death! Trees look like trees for a long time after they die, and dead bugs look like bugs for months after taking their last tiny breaths. But dogs left to rot . . . No reason to get into the gruesome details.

My brother kept pushing. "This will be our greatest experiment yet! And we'll know once and for all if the lightning ball works on animals. Plus it's Scruffy. Wouldn't it be great to have him back? He was so much fun!"

"If it works, it won't be Scruffy that comes back," I said, "not *our* Scruffy. It would be zombie Scruffy, or something just as freaky."

Fenton showed a sick smile. "Zombie Scruffy could also work." He kept needling, and I knew that further protests on my part would be useless. You see, we had loved that stupid dog. And even if there was only a one-in-a-million chance that Scruffy could be restored by the ball of light—well, that was something you could talk me into trying.

Chapter 8

Operation Dig Up Scruffy

Minutes after finishing dessert, Fenton and I stood in the animal graveyard near the outbuilding. It was kind of a busy place—a lot of death happens on farms. Its residents included Scruffy, a cat named Fiskers, a run-over chicken, a duck that died of old age, a lizard, a gerbil, and a goldfish named Goldie Fish. Scruffy, the most loved of them all, had the biggest cross.

I held two shovels, and in my pocket was Dad's camera. Fenton clutched the jar with the light ball in it. The ground was muddy from the storm. It wasn't dark yet, but it was getting there.

"How are we going to do this?" I asked. "Scruffy won't fit inside the jar."

Clearly, Fenton hadn't thought about logistics. He chewed on his lip. "Let's start digging and we'll figure it out later."

He set the jar down. I handed a shovel to him and we went to work.

"I have a bad feeling about this," I said, wondering if digging up a dead pet was a moral issue, like it would be if it was a person. The saying is "Rest in peace," not "Rest in peace until two dopey kids dig you up."

We were shoveling muddy dirt when I looked at the jar and saw the light ball bouncing wildly against the glass like it was trying to get out.

"Look," I said. "The ball of light wants to escape!"

Fenton saw what I was seeing, the light ball pushing against the jar like a trapped animal wanting to break out of its cage. The ball was pulsing fast, like its life depended on it getting out of there. Maybe it was suffocating! I hadn't made any air holes in the lid.

"I think we should let it go," I said. "It looks miserable. It might even be dying."

"That's a terrible idea," Fenton said. "We need to keep it inside the jar until we figure out how to use it on Scruffy. Besides, it's lightning. How could it be dying?"

"It just is! Can't you see it? It really wants out of the jar."

"Fiona, ignore it and keep digging."

But I couldn't ignore it, just like I couldn't ignore a wolf or a coyote trying to break free of a leg trap. Watching the light ball bounce against the glass, I had a sudden sense that there was a big reason it wanted to be let out. I also knew that I was about to risk my brother's wrath and a fist to my arm by trying to free it.

So I snatched up the barrel jar, turning away from Fenton so he could not stop me, though he tried. "Give that to me!" he demanded. "Don't you dare let it go!" As he grabbed at my arms I twisted off the lid and said to the light, "Go! You are free!" The light ball shot out of the jar and zipped toward the clouds like it had been punted. I soon lost sight of it.

Uh-oh. The light ball didn't want to help Fenton and me dig up Scruffy, it just wanted to return to the sky, which was probably where it lived. And now my brother was going to whomp me.

"What did you do *that* for?" he said, pushing me away. "I told you to not let it out. You ruined everything!"

Trying to ignore Fenton's tirade, which I feared would go on for days, I picked up my shovel and was planning to go back to the house, when a flash of light lit up the sky, so bright I shielded my eyes. The great ball of light zoomed back to earth like it was fired from a cannon.

"Here it comes!" I shouted.

But as the light got closer, it seemed to be aiming for Fenton and me, like it was mad at us for keeping it in a jar and was out for revenge.

Instead of saving my butt, I froze; I literally was incapable of moving. When the streaking ball was just about on us, Fenton said, "Get out of the way, dummy!" and flung an arm around me and threw us to the ground. We landed hard in mud.

As my brother and I pushed ourselves out of the muck, we saw the light ball strike Scruffy's grave with perfect aim—and then it burrowed inside it!

Fenton and I clambered to our feet and wiped mud off our faces, and saw the soil above Scruffy's grave begin to move, just a little. Fenton grabbed my arm.

And then the ground rumbled, mini-earthquake style.

And then the light ball launched itself out of the grave and rolled until it came to rest right beside the jar. I tilted the jar, and the light ball slipped inside it like a well-behaved pet. Strangely, the ball was free of mud, like it had a built-in self-cleaning mechanism.

"What . . . what the heck just happened?" Fenton asked, confounded.

"No idea," I said. "But it was kind of cool, wasn't it?"

I pulled out the camera, aimed it at the grave, and began filming in video mode. It was quiet for several seconds, but then more dirt moved, and now I grabbed Fenton's arm. A few inches of a dog paw emerged from the grave, but it was nearly all bone, with just a tiny patch of fur.

"Oh. My. God," said Fenton, watching the skeleton paw push away dirt. "Maybe this wasn't . . . um . . . such a good idea?"

Say what?

A second paw rose out of the mud—just bone. Scruffy was digging himself out of his grave! I didn't know whether to run away screaming or shout encouragement, but I did keep filming until the batteries died.

Soon we saw part of Scruffy's snout pop out of the dirt—just bone. I shoved the camera into my pocket and picked up my shovel.

"What are you doing?" Fenton asked.

"If he attacks me, I'm going to defend myself," I said, unsure if I could use the shovel on Scruffy, even if he became violent. My brother didn't say anything, but he picked up his shovel too.

Scruffy's digging became stronger, and he slowly emerged from his grave, first his head and part of his body and then the rest of him. When he finally was upright, he shook off dirt clods and his tailbone went flying.

It was the creepiest thing I had ever seen. Scruffy was about 85 percent skeleton, 10 percent gray flesh, and 5 percent white fur. It looked like his internal organs had rotted away. He only had one eye, and it wasn't completely attached. Most of his teeth were gone, except for a fang and three regular teeth. No tongue. No most other stuff that normally comprises a dog.

And there was the smell, wafting toward my brother and me and forcing us to cover our noses. I started gagging.

Fenton, looking like he was about to be sick, somehow held it in and cautiously stepped closer to Scruffy. "Hey, boy. Hey, Scruffy." He hesitantly held out his hand—it was shaking. "Remember us? Fenton and Fiona. We used to run around and play together every day."

Scruffy searched for the source of the sound, causing me to suspect that he was mostly blind, then he went through the motions of barking, though only a high-pitched, ear-hurting squeal came out of his mouth. If he remembered Fenton and me, he sure didn't seem happy to see us again.

"You try," my brother said, looking at me.

I put the shovel behind my back so I wouldn't appear dangerous. "Scruffy? This is Fiona. I just wanted to say, uh, um . . . welcome back to the world!"

Scruffy squealed again and snapped his jaw, causing me to jump back. It was pretty pathetic. He was one tenth of a dog trying to act like a full dog.

"This isn't right, and that's not Scruffy," I said to my brother, keeping an eye on the dog. "We need to send him back." That was the correct plan, I thought, but I didn't want to be the one whacking Scruffy on the head with a shovel and then reburying him.

"We can't do that," said Fenton. "For the sake of science we need to keep Scruffy around and observe him and see how long he lives, and if there are any changes over time."

"What kinds of changes?"

"Like, I don't know, if he grows some fur and teeth and everything else that he's missing. Oh. And if he starts looking and acting more like a real dog." He told me to keep an eye on Scruffy (I already was!) while he ran inside for his collar and chain, which we had kept for purely sentimental reasons.

As I gazed at Scruffy, it seemed like everything good and loving about him was gone, and all that was left was a shell of a dog squealing at me as if I were a stranger who he no longer recognized as a friend. I asked myself if I had the courage to do what was right and send him back but could only spit out a feeble "Maybe."

I raised the shovel. "You have to do this, Fiona," I told myself. "You have to be strong." I peered at the skeleton dog. "I'm sorry, Scruffy, I really am. Good-bye."

Just as I was about to close my eyes and do the terrible deed, I saw something that gave me pause: Scruffy dragged a paw across his snout like he had often done when he was alive. Somewhere in that hideous creature was Scruffy, *my Scruffy*, even though he was missing his soul and fifty other important things.

"Oh Scruffy," I said.

I lowered the shovel and broke out in tears as a flood of memories kicked in.

Like the day Dad gave Scruffy to Fenton and me, and our hilarious efforts to give him a bath.

Like all the cuddling I used to do with Scruffy, on the couch or living room floor while watching TV, and on a blanket when Fenton, Scruffy, and I would have a picnic near the barn (we had a strict no cats, goats, ducks, or chickens policy).

Like how Scruffy would sometimes confuse instructions, barking when Fenton or I said "sit," and sitting when one of us said "bark." He was the dumbest dog ever!

Like running through a cornfield with Scruffy, the stalks taller than we were, both of us so happy we were yipping.

Looking at the poor dog now as he rested on his haunches, I knew that I would never do anything to harm him. I never hurt him when he was alive-alive, so why would I when he was alive-dead? He had been a good and loyal friend once. A tiny spark of hope burned inside me that, despite Scruffy's significant deadness and decay, we could somehow be friends again.

Chapter 9

There's a Hellhound in the Storm Cellar

It took Fenton five minutes of trial and error and near calamity to slip the leather collar on Scruffy. Until then the skeleton dog squealed and snapped at him. The breakthrough came when I distracted Scruffy by chirping and quacking and making a fool of myself. When the dog looked at me, Fenton snuck the collar over him without getting bitten.

After talking it over, we decided to keep Scruffy in the storm cellar. Dad never went in there unless bad storms were threatening. "I feel like we've messed with stuff that shouldn't be messed with," I said to Fenton as he led Scruffy by his chain away from his grave.

"It's called science," he said. "I thought you liked science."

"Not this kind of science," I said. What kind of science did I like? The science of cloud making and rock formation and butterfly migration and ant colonies. What kind didn't I like? The kind involving corpses and skeletons and zombie pets, which was the exact kind of science we had going on here.

As we walked through the farmyard, the other animals gave a wide berth to Scruffy. The chickens stopped cackling. A duck flew out of the way. Daisy freaked out and ran faster than I had ever seen a goat run before. And Screech the cat hissed and threw a claw at Scruffy, before skedaddling under the porch. None of the animals recognized the skeleton dog as their old pal Scruffy.

While Fenton led Scruffy into the cellar, I ran inside the house for fresh batteries for the camera and for my science notebook, as well as for some of Scruffy's old chew toys that we had saved, you guessed it, for sentimental reasons.

In the cellar I set the toys on the floor near Scruffy. He just stared at them for a little while, then he began chewing on a rubber bone with a broken squeaker. I had figured he'd go for the tiny football. During his first life it was his favorite toy.

"He's acting a little more like the old Scruffy, don't you think?" said Fenton, hopeful.

"Not really," I said, still regretting bringing Scruffy back. But, being a good scientist, I wrote down some observations about the latest sideways miracle, the skeleton dog living in our storm cellar, and took pictures and shot some video that, if I posted it on YouTube, would cause one billion people to pee their pants.

My brother was hunkered down beside the hellhound. "Do you remember, boy, chasing after sticks and balls I threw, and then bringing them back to me so I could toss them again?" he said in a soft voice, like he was talking to a frightened child. "Do you remember any of that fun stuff we did?"

It didn't work. Scruffy ignored him and chewed the rubber bone. And I wondered if any memories of his first life existed somewhere inside Scruffy. Or was he starting from scratch?

It was a school night and it was getting late, so we said good night to Scruffy, Fenton adding, "I love you, you stupid horrible dog." I considered saying something similar, but I couldn't talk myself into it. I had loved the real Scruffy, but loving . . . *this* . . . would take some time.

Chapter 10

The Undeniable Holiness of Blueberry Pancakes

The single good thing about our dad spending so many hours at the Ice Queen's house was that the next day he usually went all out fixing breakfast for Fenton and me, probably due to guilt from leaving us alone for much of the night. So we woke up to find he was making blueberry pancakes and cheesy scrambled eggs, and he'd picked up pineapple-orange juice for us to drink.

"A meal fit for royalty," Dad said, flipping a pancake on the griddle as my brother and I set out silverware and napkins.

I was glad for the boost of energy provided by the wholesome eats, because I hadn't gotten much sleep the night before. Fenton and I had agreed that I would keep the light ball hidden in my room since Dad hardly ever went in there. I'm not sure what it is about men and boys and their fear of all things girl, including their rooms. What are they expecting? A trick floor? A monster in the closet? Germs?

I set the barrel jar on my desk, but after I said my prayers and turned off the lamp, the ball was shooting out so much light I had to move it to the closet and put a blanket over it. My room went mostly dark, just a sliver of light sneaking out of the bottom of the closet door.

What kept me awake for another couple of hours was not the light, but my tangled thoughts about what exactly that ball of light was, and what it might be capable of beyond bringing a tree and bugs and a dog back to life. Was the ball some kind of holy force, I wondered, the stuff the universe used to create life out of a mishmash of chemicals? Or was it something else?

And why, of all the places in the universe it could visit, did it show up on my farm in Montana? I considered the possibility that its appearance at Bluebird Acres was as random as a lightning strike, but I kept thinking about how the light rolled back into the jar after waking up Scruffy. It seemed to be cooperating with Fenton and me, like it was a third member of our science team.

I looked at the dimmed glow coming from my closet, hoping it would send forth some answers, but none came. But isn't that true with the big questions of life, that they only seed more questions instead of providing answers?

We were almost finished with breakfast, and Dad hadn't said anything about the miracle tree, so I thought I should mention it and maybe keep him from spazzing out if he hadn't seen it yet.

"So Dad," I said, trying to look casual, "did you see the tree in the front yard, the one that got struck by lightning during the storm? It's pretty weird what happened to it." I looked at Fenton and saw nervousness in his eyes.

"Did it catch fire?" Dad asked, sawing through a pancake. "I probably should have cut it down after it died, but I just couldn't talk myself into it. Your uncle Jack and I spent half our summers in that tree when we were kids."

"No . . . it didn't catch fire," I said, worry narrowing my throat. "Maybe you should go take a look."

He finished chewing a bite of pancake, then went

into the living room and peered out the picture window. I jumped up and shadowed him. Fenton, whose life is dedicated to eating, stayed at the table and finished his breakfast.

"I don't believe it," Dad said, his eyes huge. "I've never seen anything like it."

Before I could speak, he was out the screen door and hurrying to the maple tree. I trotted after him as he circled the tree again and again, finally touching the bark and then some leaves that were shaped in the weird way maple leaves are shaped.

Dad was getting emotional, and so was I. The tree had meant something to my father when it was alive, and now it meant something again. It made me think about the things we attached ourselves to: people and pets we loved, toys we enjoyed playing with, and books we liked reading. And even a tree we once climbed and carved our initials into.

"How is it possible that a lightning strike could do this?" he asked, like I was a renowned expert on these matters. "Maybe I should call the newspaper and tell them about it—they'd write an article about this! Or bring in some science guys from the University of Montana to take a look and figure out what happened. Just wait until I tell your uncle Jack!"

Oh boy. I didn't like the direction this was heading.

"I have a theory," I said, and then I quickly came up with a theory: the tree had not been dead, even though it looked dead, but instead it had been dormant these past few years, and the lightning strike woke it up and caused it to shoot out new leaves. That was not what I believed, but I said all that to my dad to keep him from letting the world know what had happened to our tree. It was too soon to go public with the miracles—Fenton and I had just begun experimenting.

"Huh. I never heard of that kind of thing happening before," Dad said, giving a leaf a gentle tug, as if to test that it was really real. I could tell he was skeptical (my dad's not dumb), so I offered to ask my science teacher at school, Mr. Embry, whether a lightning strike causing a "dead-looking" tree to grow new leaves was rare, or not, and then we'd decide what to do.

Dad agreed but spent another ten minutes with the maple tree, like he was looking for proof that the whole thing was a con job instead of, well, an absolute miracle.

Before getting ready for school, Fenton and I had to feed and water the animals and make sure they were all accounted for, except the cats, which were free to come and go.

After setting out food pellets for the goats, I checked on Scruffy in the storm cellar. I wondered if he had been upset, locked away all night. The "real" Scruffy always slept at the foot of my bed or Fenton's bed. But he was right where we'd left him, chewing on the rubber bone, and I wondered if he had been doing that all night—did a skeleton dog need to sleep? Then it struck me: Did he eat? Drink? And where would food and water go, now that most of his innards were gone?

"I'm sorry," I said to Scruffy, as guilt for bringing him back tugged at me. "Sometimes awful things happen in the name of science."

He ignored me. I was about to leave when a memory squiggled to the surface.

"Do you remember," I said to Scruffy, "that each morning when Fenton and I climbed inside the school bus and it took off, how you would run alongside for a while before giving up? And then in the afternoon you would wait by the road until you saw the bus, and come running up and give us some love as soon as we stepped off it? Do you remember any of that stuff, Scruffy?"

He looked up, squealed in that horrible high-pitched way and showed his few teeth, and went back to chewing the bone.

"The heck with you," I said, stamping away. It was like Scruffy wasn't even trying to be a good and lovable dog. But then I remembered that it wasn't my dog's fault if his soul and memories were gone, so I cooled down a little.

Chapter 11

Fenton Gets a Big Head

After kissing Dad good-bye, Fenton and I lumbered to the road, backpacks slung on our shoulders, to wait for the bus. Standing there in bright sunlight, we made a pact to not tell anyone—not even our friends—about the light ball, until it was time to go public with our discovery. We bumped fists to make it official.

"You know something, Fiona?" Fenton said, kicking at gravel. "I feel different than I did yesterday."

I checked his face. "Oh my gosh, you have a third eye and four noses. You *are* different!"

"Ha! That's not what I meant. It's just . . . Well, now that I've brought some stuff back to life—with your help—it's like I'm a different person than I used to be. I guess I feel, I don't know, more important."

"Cool," I answered. What I was thinking was *Here's something new and different*. Fenton already could get a little prideful and self-important, and now having the power over life (at least with crickets and dogs) was going to swell up his head even more than it already was. Like our mom said when she lived with us, leave pride to lions, and vanity to mirrors.

But as I thought it over, I realized that I also felt different, though in a confused, *what's next* kind of way—no big-headedness involved. Fenton and I had crossed a line that maybe no other kid in the history of the world had crossed. So what was the reasonable next step? More experiments with the light ball? Try to ditch it before things got further out of control? Or hand over the light ball to Dad and confess everything? That morning I had only questions, buzzing around my head like bees. A solid answer or two would have been nice.

As the bus pulled away from our farm, I peered at the miracle tree and felt all warm inside. Green life was so much prettier than rotten death, and even though it was all the ball of light's doing, it felt like I had helped in a big win for the good guys. I hoped that the new life would last awhile.

There were only two other kids on the bus, though it would slowly fill up as we moved closer to Red Lodge. Before it became too noisy, I found myself thinking about my mom and what she was doing. I imagined her inside her Manhattan apartment, maybe drinking an espresso and eating a bagel with cream cheese on it—her favorite breakfast. Maybe in her head she was planning her next article, a story about celebrity tattoos, let's say.

Or maybe—and here was where hope snuck in and planted a few daisies—she was thinking about Fenton and me and making plans to phone us, or even fly out that weekend for a surprise visit. Stupid, huh? She barely called once a week.

Even stupider, I can't tell you how much I wanted to ask the driver to stop the bus so I could jump out, run to the nearest house, beg to use the phone, and call my mom to tell her about the light ball. *That* might keep her on the phone! Oh, who was I kidding? She'd still find an excuse to end the call: *my editor is on the other line—have to fly! Smooches!*

Insert miserable sigh.

The big difference between my mom and dad is that if I said to them that a spaceship had crash-landed in the cornfield and three-headed aliens were running

amok on the farm, my mom would huff disappoint-
edly and tell me to save my imagination for my short
stories, while my dad, even if he did not believe me,
would take my hand, grab a pitchfork in case the
aliens became violent, and say, "Let's go investigate
the crash site and then have ourselves an alien barbecue." And we'd make a fun half hour out of it.

Dad rocks. Mom, not so much.

The last stop before we crossed into Red Lodge
was to pick up the Stambaugh kids, Luke and Emily.
For most of my school life I was friends with Emily,
who was my age, but then I became closer with Luke,
who was one year older. I still liked Emily, but one
day about a year ago she decided that she'd rather
hang out with prep girls, and that just wasn't me. We
still said hi to each other, but she had her friends and
I had mine.

Luke, on the other hand—I was pretty sure he liked
me in a boy-girl kind of way. Sometimes he'd trip me
when we walked down school halls, and if we sat
together on the bus he made sure our shoes or our
knees "accidentally" touched. It was all very sweet,
and even though I wasn't old enough to date boys yet,
I never minded the sneaker and knee love.

That morning, like usual, Luke plunked down

next to me. "Hey, Fiona, what's new?" he said, flicking blond bangs from his eyes as the bus drove away from his house. It was pretty awesome how he did that bang-flicking thing so smoothly.

"Nothing," I said. *Why was he asking me this?* "Why? Did you hear that something was new?"

"No, but that's what we do. I ask you if anything is new and you say no, then you ask me if anything is new and I say no, and then we ride in silence the rest of the way to school. It's our thing!"

"Sorry," I said, my face going red. Now I understood what "paranoid" meant. "I'll get it right tomorrow."

Just so you know, Luke isn't a huge part of this story. But I like the kid, and it didn't seem right to not include him in a book about my life. I hope that's okay.

Cosmological Monkeys

My major complaint about Roosevelt Middle School is that my class schedule was planned by monkeys. For example, gym happened right after lunch, which could not be good for digestion, especially considering some of the "food" they pass off as lunch. (I'm certain that the cheese they use in the veggie lasagna is 40 percent Frisbee-grade plastic.)

Even stupider, library study hall was scheduled for second period, so it was of little use when it came to completing homework that had been assigned that day. Usually I spent the forty minutes doing some reading. But that morning I went searching for my science teacher, Mr. Embry, so I could hammer him with

questions. I found him in the science section looking at a book about microbiology while on break between classes. Mr. Embry was forty-two or forty-three, practically Precambrian, and liked to wear bow ties and funny-looking socks with geometric patterns on them.

"Hello again, Fiona," he said. "What cosmological conundrums are bugging you today?"

One reason I liked Mr. Embry was that he not only knew stuff, he *knew stuff.* In other words he was kind of deep. And he was one of those teachers who pushed his students to come up with their own answers instead of looking at the back of the book or going online, and he was always saying inspiring stuff like "Live life to the max, even if your name isn't Max." I sometimes wondered why a person with such a lively mind was working at Roosevelt Middle. There were, I want to say, some bits of sadness detectable in Mr. Embry's eyes, like maybe something was missing from his life. Sure, teaching science is a totally awesome thing to do, but maybe it was not the best thing possible for a man like Mr. Embry?

"Actually, I do have a few questions for you," I said. "Here's one! Can lightning come in ball form, or are bolts and flashes the only options?"

He gave me his full attention. "It's difficult to

answer that question with authority. All I can say is that throughout history there have been reports of lightning balls, but it's a rare phenomenon, and no one knows exactly why lightning might occasionally appear in ball form, if in fact it has. I don't think there is irrefutable evidence one way or the other."

"But if ball lightning has sometimes happened," I said, feeling a little prickly underneath my skin, which sometimes occurs when I'm thinking extra hard about stuff, "what could have caused it?"

"I'm not sure, but my guess is that those folks saw something other than a lightning ball," he said. "It could have been Saint Elmo's fire, or some sort of electromagnetic disturbance caused by forces we don't completely understand. And of course with some of the reports it's possible that the viewer of the alleged lightning ball was hallucinating, or perhaps they made up the story to draw attention to themselves."

That was a little mean, accusing people of being liars and hallucinators.

"Has anyone ever caught lightning, like, say, in a big glass jar?" I asked.

Mr. Embry tapped an index finger against his chin. "I don't think it would be possible—lightning only lasts for a split second. As far as lightning balls go, there have been reports of them lasting up to a minute, but even if someone had thought to trap it inside a jar or another container, and they didn't get electrocuted or burned, it would not stick around very long."

"Why?"

"Because lightning is an electrical discharge, and electrical discharges quickly peter out."

"Okay, thanks," I said, piecing together what Mr. Embry had told me with the reality of the light ball and the miracles it caused. It was a lousy fit, like trying to jam a house key into a locker lock.

My teacher searched the shelves for a book about lightning and handed it to me. "I have a question for *you*," he said. "Why are you asking about lightning balls? Did you see something that you thought might be one?"

"No," I said, averting my eyes so he would not see that they were of the lying kind. "I had a dream last night, probably because of the storm, where light balls were bouncing around my farm. I was just wondering if something like that could happen in real life."

"At least you have interesting dreams," he said.

"I dreamed last night that I was at McDonald's and ordered a hamburger, but it came with one pickle slice instead of two. I was furious."

Talk about getting off track. I said good-bye to Mr. Embry, then took the lightning book to a study carrel. It was all very interesting, but by the time I reached the end of the book I was nearly certain that Fenton and I had caught something other than lightning.

Chapter 13

Scruffy 2.0

The first thing Fenton and I did after school was check on Scruffy. He was waiting for us at the storm cellar doors. As soon as Fenton opened the doors, the skeleton dog climbed the steps and trotted away, dragging his chain.

"Where do you think he's going?" my brother asked. I didn't have a clue.

But Scruffy knew. He led us to the animal graveyard, then he dropped down on his grave and pawed at the dirt, like he wanted to get back in.

"He wants to go home," I said, feeling like I had been punched in the stomach.

"That can't be true," Fenton said, his voice pained. "Something must be wrong."

"What's wrong is that we didn't give him the option of coming back or staying put. We just . . . forced it on him! And hoped for the best!" I pointed at Scruffy. "But we didn't get the best. We got that horrible . . . thing."

Scruffy dug at the dirt. It was disturbing, seeing an animal digging his own grave.

"I'll go get the shovels," I said. "We can help him."

"No!" Fenton said with a burst of anger. "We have to keep Scruffy around. The experiment isn't over yet!"

"Science isn't everything, Fenton," I said.

"I know. But maybe Scruffy, in time, will start liking the world again and want to stay. It's worth a shot, isn't it?"

I looked at the poor dog and thought about how, in olden days, he loved to chase a soccer ball (or any moving object, really)—I wanted to see him that happy again. I sighed loudly, so Fenton would know I was making a big decision here.

"I guess it's worth a shot," I said. "But if he keeps wanting to go back to his grave, one of these days we have to let him."

Fenton nodded fast, then grabbed Scruffy's chain and pulled him away from the graveyard. That raised another moral issue: we were keeping an animal from doing something he wanted to do. Why did people assume they had the right to decide what animals could and could not do?

"Go get your soccer ball," my brother said while dragging Scruffy. "I have an idea. And for once could you just go along with it instead of asking a million irritating questions first?"

I hissed, but really it was like Fenton had read my mind a minute ago, and even if that kind of thing happens with twins a lot, that doesn't make it less jarring: it's *my* mind! Keep out!

Anyway.

I ran inside and found the ball. Fenton had coaxed Scruffy into the backyard. He tied him to a clothesline post—we didn't want him to head back to the grave—then he and I kicked the ball to each other. A few minutes passed, and the plan didn't seem to be working—Scruffy didn't even look at us. I found myself getting increasingly dejected. I'd really hoped that as soon as the soccer ball rolled past Scruffy he would become a real dog again and pounce at it.

Enough.

"Your experiment failed," I said. *Stupid idea. Stupid!* "I've got homework to do."

"A few more kicks," my brother insisted. "Three!"

"Okay, fine. But then I'm done."

And then a tiny miracle occurred. On the second kick the soccer ball rolled past Scruffy, and he padded up to it and nudged it along a few inches with his snout, like how he used to do when he was alive. He then dropped down on the grass and barked in that obnoxious squealing way.

"Yes!" Fenton said. "That's a good sign, don't you think? He sort of played!"

"We'll see." I'm normally an easy hoper, but I was slamming the brakes on that big hope. Scruffy 2.0 was nowhere close to being a real dog yet.

We kicked the ball by him a few more times. He squealed, but seemed exhausted by his big nose nudge and didn't do it again.

"We better put him back in the storm cellar," I said. "He seems wiped out, plus what if a neighbor sees him?"

So we returned him to the cellar. There, Scruffy pounced on his rubber bone and chewed it. Happy again, I guess.

Bad Science, Bad Lies, Bad Plans

Inside the house, Fenton and I checked to make sure the ball of light was snug in the barrel jar, then we broke off in different directions, my brother wanting to do more science experiments with the light ball, while I needed to complete a homework assignment for American History: twenty-five pages plus a six-paragraph essay in one night. Totally unfair!

I had just started reading about the Mexican-American War, and something called "manifest destiny," when Fenton yelled, "Fiona! Get in here!" Now what? Had the formerly dead worm morphed into a rattlesnake and eaten the insects?

Fenton was in his doorway, half in, half out, and totally frozen, except for his right hand, which was

shakily pointing at the dead field mouse he had gutted a week earlier. It was hopping around the room! Now I froze. The mouse jumped, would land somewhere, spastically shake for several seconds, then zing off again. The poor mouse was out of control.

"What the heck?" I eventually said.

"It was just an experiment!" my brother cried. "I wasn't expecting *this*. Besides, it's the lightning ball's fault, not mine. All I did was, um, drop the dead mouse inside the jar."

I watched the light ball as it throbbed indifferently, as if to say, *Hey, I only bring stuff back, it's up to you to deal with the messes.* Meanwhile, the spastic mouse landed on a bookshelf, threw itself against a wall, landed upside down on the rug, shook for several seconds, and flung itself against the closet door.

"What are we going to do?" I asked. "We can't have a dead mouse flying around the house. Dad will see it for sure."

Fenton groaned. "I guess I should kill it. Put it out of its misery."

"Alright," I said. "But first let me shoot some video. For the sake of science!"

I left the room and got Dad's camera. When I returned, Fenton was already clutching his baseball bat, ready to smash the undead mouse.

I shot some video and narrated, "Here we have a clear example of good scientific intentions gone bad," then I nodded at Fenton. He crept up to the mouse as it trembled on the carpet, then he swung the bat, but the mouse zinged out of the way and splatted against a

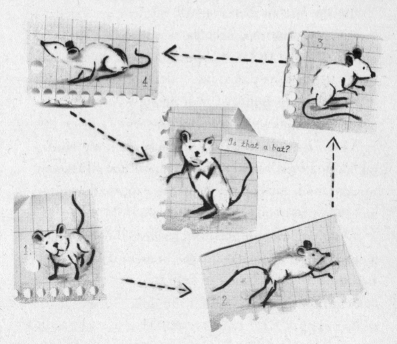

chair before tumbling to the floor. Poor mouse!

My brother was about to take another swing when I put up a hand to stop him.

"Wait," I said, softening. "I don't think it wants to die. It's jumping out of the way to save itself, just like a living mouse would."

Fenton ignored me and swung the bat; this time the mouse jumped sideways and landed on the desk. My brother swung again, but instead of the mouse he hit a ceramic lamp and shattered the base. Meanwhile the mouse was spazzing on the rug.

My brother dropped the bat.

"Please don't tell Dad about the lamp," he pleaded, trying to stick the pieces back together. "I don't want to pay for a new one. I'm poor enough already."

I glared at him—I'd told him to stop.

"Okay, I won't tell," I said finally, "as long as you quit trying to kill the mouse." My brother reluctantly agreed, and I came up with a plan to capture the mouse in a pillowcase and release it outside.

It took a few minutes, but eventually the mouse jumped into the pillowcase as I held it open, almost as if it knew I was trying to help it. I set it free at the edge of the cornfield.

"Good luck with your second life," I said to the

mouse. "And, uh, I'm sorry that my brother gutted you. He's weird that way."

Watching the mouse hop and roll and stumble away between young cornstalks, I thought that the instinct for self-preservation was pretty powerful—it might not even require a brain or major organs. The mouse had none of that stuff, and yet he clearly did not want to be smashed by a baseball bat. Every life values itself, I guess, even if we don't value it.

And then I headed back to Fenton's room. He'd already sort of shoved the lamp back together and was hiding the cracked base with a pile of comic books.

"Listen closely," he said, looking up, "because you may never hear these words again: you were right and I was wrong. We shouldn't have captured the lightning ball, or done any of the experiments. But we did do all of that, and now everything is messed up."

"I understand," I said evenly, but inside I was gloating. Fenton admitting that I was right and he was wrong almost *never* happens. Once every three years, tops.

He handed the barrel jar to me and said to not let him have it until further notice. Clearly, the mouse thing had really freaked him out.

I hid the jar inside my closet, but before covering it with a blanket I had that sense again that there was a reason the light ball had come into our yard and was allowing us to conduct our experiments.

"Why are you here?" I said to it, but all it did was glow and pulse and give me a fresh dose of the heebie-jeebies.

I was finishing my essay on manifest destiny when I heard Dad's car coming up the driveway.

It's a funny thing, the sounds we tie our feelings to, like the gravel-crunching sound of my father pulling his car close to the house. I would bet you ten dollars that if we did an experiment where I was blindfolded and had to listen to a hundred cars including my dad's SUV come up my driveway and stop, I could pick out the one car I had ridden in and the one driver who I loved.

I was eager to give Dad a big hug, but a few minutes had passed and he hadn't come inside. So I went to the picture window and saw him standing next to the miracle tree, touching a leaf and saying something.

I ran outside and gave him that big hug.

"I was thinking about the maple tree so often I was having trouble focusing on work today," he said as we separated. "I told a guy I was working with about the tree, and he said I was crazy, that lightning couldn't bring a dead tree back to life. I invited him to come out to the farm to see for himself, but I don't think he will." He laughed and added, "I'm pretty sure he thought I was drunk."

"You, uh, know something, Dad?" I said. "It might not be a good idea to tell people about the tree. The goats, they get really upset when strangers visit our farm." I then launched the lie I had cobbled together, saying I had spoken to a science teacher at my school, and he said that there were other known cases of a lightning strike causing a "deadish" tree to come alive again.

"Mr. Embry told me that sometimes a tree looks dead, but actually there's still life going on inside it," I said. "And when lightning hits it, that little bit of life that's left sort of wakes up in a jolt and causes the tree to grow new leaves."

I was expecting my dad to give me a skeptical look, but instead he said that even if it had happened before, that did not take away from the amazing fact that it had happened to our tree on our farm. "It's like we have been visited by grace, or something spiritual like that," he said. He slung an arm around me and we walked to the house.

While Dad fixed dinner—it was taco night—he told Fenton and me that he had phoned Uncle Jack and told him about the tree, and he was planning to drive down from Great Falls that Saturday to see it, and then we'd all head over to Grandma Jean's apartment in Red Lodge for a visit.

"Cool," I said, watching Fenton make a funny face as he set out drinking glasses and a carton of milk. My brother and I loved Grandma Jean—we did!—but that didn't mean we enjoyed spending time with her. She mostly watched TV and didn't say much, like she forgot we were there. Dad told us that his mom used to be more "with it" when Grandpa Wade was alive, but ever since he died she had "shut down emotionally."

The way I figured it, it was like my grandmother was waiting to die so she could be with Grandpa Wade again, and it made me mad and it was hard to watch. Life is already short, so why not try to live your days and months and years as best as possible while you can? My grandpa wasted his life by getting drunk and crashing into a tree and dying. And now my grandma was wasting her life in a different way, even though she still had my dad and Fenton and me to keep her company.

I did not understand it. And I didn't know how to fix it either.

Chapter 15

Uncle Jack

Uncle Jack got here at about one o'clock on Saturday. Fenton and I were hoping that he would surprise us and show up with a girlfriend, but that didn't happen. We've been trying to marry off Jack for the longest time so that we might one day have cousins to play with, but so far no luck.

After Uncle Jack climbed out of his Subaru, and Fenton, Dad, and I survived his bone-crushing hugs, Dad brought him right over to the miracle tree.

"I thought you were pulling my leg, telling me the old maple tree had come back to life," Uncle Jack said. "But, jeez, it really is alive again." He touched a branch and a leaf, then pulled out his cell phone and took pictures of the tree from different angles.

I wasn't too happy about Uncle Jack snapping photos of the tree. What if he posted them online and scientists and reporters saw them? Our farm could be crawling with people wanting to see and touch the miracle tree, and then it could get out of control, and people would come here for cures for their runny nose, or whatever. I could see it now, the Bluebird Acres Holy Shrine and Gift Shop.

But I couldn't think of a way to stop Uncle Jack from taking pictures that did not involve stomping on his phone. So I repeated the lie that my science teacher had told me that this was not the first time a lightning strike had "activated" a tree that appeared to be dead. My hope was that a less impressed Jack would keep the photos, and story, to himself.

"I don't care if it's happened a thousand times before," he said, reviewing the photos he had taken. "The fact that it happened to this tree, *our* old tree, is nothing but amazing."

He put away the phone and told a story about how when he and Dad were kids the maple tree was one of their sanctuaries when Grandpa Wade was drunk and yelling nasty things, since Grandpa Wade was forbidden by Grandma Jean to go outside when drunk—she didn't want the neighbors to see him stumbling around and cursing.

"Yep. We'd often head for the maple tree instead of the barn or the outbuilding," he said. "We'd climb it and hang out in the branches, and tell stories or jokes until the storm— the one going on inside our house— passed, and it was safe to return." He cocked his head, thinking. "Maybe because the tree was a living thing it was a bigger draw than the barn. Not to be goofy, but it was almost like we were being held by a giant, living hand."

"Not too goofy, I guess," Dad said, squeezing my uncle's shoulder. Dad and Uncle Jack aren't normally emotional guys, but when they dig up stories about their childhood, things can get a bit messy for all of us.

As I looked at the maple tree, I finally got why it meant so much to my dad and uncle. It wasn't just a tree they had carved their initials into and climbed and goofed around in. More, it was like an escape pod, their own little place, when Grandpa Wade was being a drunken fool and they wanted to get away from him. The tree had been a good friend when they needed a friend the most. So in that way it was already a miracle tree long before it died and was reborn.

A few minutes later we packed ourselves into Uncle Jack's car and drove to Grandma Jean's apartment building in Red Lodge. It was a sunny day, but when he pulled into the parking lot it was like gray clouds swooped in and blocked the sun, even though in real life that didn't happen.

"Can I wait in the car?" Fenton asked with futility, since he knew that Dad would not allow it.

"You guys will survive spending a few hours with your grandmother," Dad said. He opened his door, though not eagerly. "She's not going to be around forever. Enjoy these times while you can."

Fenton and I traded doomed looks, certain that nothing enjoyable was going to happen during our visit.

Inside the building, Dad knocked on the door and we waited for Grandma Jean to answer. I jokingly considered yelling, *Run for your lives, everyone!*—but didn't. Still, it sounded like a great idea.

When Grandma Jean finally opened the door she wore a confused look, like she was wondering what we were doing there. So Dad reminded her that he had phoned her two days earlier to say that we would be stopping by on Saturday for a visit.

"Is it someone's birthday?" she asked.

"No birthdays today," Dad said. "We came to visit you because we love you and miss you."

If this were a different family, I'll even say a better family, the grandmother might have said, *I love you guys too and miss you so much!* And then she'd give everyone hugs and warm kisses, and we'd feel her love roll through us and settle in our toes.

Instead Grandma Jean patted us on the back as we stepped inside, like we were on the same soccer team and she was our coach. *Good job, guys.* Some kids complained when relatives kissed them or pinched their faces like they were made out of clay. I thought of those kids as the lucky ones.

My grandmother had a hundred TV channels to choose from, but for some reason she was watching an infomercial for fish-oil supplements. After we sat down, Dad sort of nudged me with his eyes, so I asked Grandma Jean how she was doing and if anything was new.

"Just getting through my days," she said heavily.

Grandma didn't ask us what was new or how we were doing, but Dad started talking anyway, saying that he had been busy with handyman jobs, and then Uncle Jack told Grandma that he was thinking of putting a new roof on his house in Great Falls. A windstorm had torn off some shingles.

"Don't do anything you can't afford," she said to Uncle Jack, which I thought was a little bit mean, suggesting that Jack wasn't making enough money to afford a new roof, or smart enough to know what he could afford.

After about fifteen minutes of misery, Fenton elbowed me in the side, our let's-get-out-of-here cue. So I announced that he and I were going for a walk so we could get some exercise. Dad and Uncle Jack looked at us with envy as we strode to the door, and Grandma Jean cautioned us to not be noisy and upset the neighbors. Translation: don't act like kids, kids!

Outside, I soaked up sunshine and felt like dancing. Fenton's and my imprisonment had ended, though we were due back at the jail in ten minutes.

"That was totally stupid," my brother said as we walked on a perfect, dandelion-free lawn.

"I know," I said, wanting to cuss or belch loudly, or do something else obnoxious that would cause elderly spies watching us from behind drapes to curse modern kids for their rudeness. "Dad says that Grandma Jean was happier when Grandpa Wade was still around, even though he was a drunk. Do you think that's true?"

Fenton wiggled his shoulders. "Maybe she only remembers the good times with Grandpa. Isn't that what old people do, remember only the good stuff and try to forget the bad stuff?"

"That's what we all try to do," I said.

We walked between the three-story brick buildings. I wondered why none of the residents were outside enjoying the sunshine. Maybe they were all watching the fish-oil commercial.

"So I've been thinking," my brother said, and caution flags waved inside my mind: *so I've been thinking* is often Fenton's lead-in before he announces his latest risky plan. "That it would sure be nice if Grandpa Wade was here. Grandma would be happier, and Dad and Uncle Jack might be too. Heck, so would we, since visits to Grandma would no longer be like volunteering for a torture session. Plus we barely even knew Grandpa Wade before the accident."

"That's true," I said, though I was pretty sure we weren't missing much. I vaguely remembered seeing Grandpa Wade a few times at our house in Great Falls. Those memories included my grandfather getting drunk and saying mean things, even to our cats and dog. Everyone would become upset, and the day would fall apart like it had been bombed. And then an embarrassed Grandma Jean would load her drunken husband into her car and they would drive back to Deerwood. When our grandparents were gone, Dad and Uncle Jack would say things like if they didn't see their father for another ten years it would be too soon. And then six or seven months later they would try again, hoping for a better outcome. And hoping for a better Grandpa Wade, too.

"Yep," said Fenton, "it's too bad Grandpa Wade isn't alive so Grandma Jean and the rest of us could be happy. It's a shame, is what it is. A great injustice!"

I gazed at my brother and saw his mouth rise up in a devious smile. Those caution flags inside me turned into shrieking alarms.

"Fenton?" I asked. "You're not thinking of doing something stupid, are you?"

"I'm always thinking of doing something stupid," he said, kicking at a cluster of oak leaves that a storm or a squirrel must have knocked to the ground. "But it's just words. It's not like we own something that can bring back the dead. Oh wait, we do." He laughed and I wanted to punch him.

"Are you crazy? You saw what kind of shape Scruffy

was in, and he was only dead for nine months. Grandpa Wade has been dead for three years. He's probably just a pile of dust."

"Wasn't he buried in a coffin? Aren't those things airtight?"

I shrugged, unsure what Grandpa Wade was buried in, though I did know the location of his grave, in a cemetery called Rolling Brook about a mile from our farm. Our dad had let Fenton and me skip the burial since we barely knew Grandpa Wade, but we had twice been to the cemetery when Uncle Jack was in town. We would drive there, grumpily stand near Grandpa's grave for ten minutes without saying anything, and head back to the farm. I wasn't quite sure why we bothered.

I was about to wage another protest when the strangest thing happened. It was like I somehow connected to the ball of light, even though we were miles apart. I could see the light ball inside my head, and for the first time I wondered if the pulsing was some kind of secret language like Morse code, but simpler and direct to my brain.

Pulse . . . pulse . . . pulse . . . , said the light.

What are you saying to me? I said to the light ball, by telepathy, I guess, though another part of my brain was wondering if I was imagining things. But at the same time, electric tingles were squiggling around in my belly.

Pulse . . . pulse . . . pulse-pulse, the light said.

Cool, I said to the light ball, *but could you please talk in English, or give me a clue as to how to decipher the code?*

Several seconds passed, then the word "trust" popped into my mind in a flashing neon-sign kind of way. While I thought about that word, the kind of word that causes people to jump from sinking ships and to life rafts, four more words appeared inside my head: *it will be okay.*

Honestly, I have no way of knowing if the light ball was communicating with me, or I was trying to find a way to justify using it to bring back Grandpa Wade. But *trust* me when I tell you this: while I can offer no proof, I do believe it's possible that I talked with the ball of light that day, and on several occasions that followed. If you choose to not believe it, I can't blame you. I'm also full of doubt.

Anyway.

As the tingling sensation faded away, I shocked Fenton by telling him I would go along with his plan to bring back Grandpa Wade, but if that blind chicken flew into the ceiling fan, it was up to him to explain what chicken feathers were doing on the rug. (I think that's a saying, maybe not.)

He agreed and we shook hands.

"You know something, Fiona," he said as we doubled back toward Grandma Jean's building. "Sometimes you are a pretty cool sister."

Instead of saying anything, I punched him in the arm, and he punched me back. It's just something we like to do.

When we returned to the parking lot, we saw that it had been infested by a silver Volkswagen Beetle belonging to the Ice Queen—Dad's girlfriend, Beverly.

"Our bad day just got ten times worse," said Fenton, a sour look on his face.

"Make that twenty times worse," I said, matching my brother's look. If Fenton and I were superheroes, Beverly would be our mortal enemy. As it was, she was just the woman dating our dad who we did not like, and who, we were certain, did not like us. But since Dad liked her . . . Well, at least we weren't making plans to blow up her car with fireworks, or anything destructive like that. *Yet.*

THE
Ice Queen

Chapter 16

Frozen Tales of the Ice Queen

G uess what," Dad said, as Fenton and I stepped inside Grandma Jean's apartment. "Beverly brought dinner—Chinese. Isn't that a nice surprise?"

"What-*ever*," Fenton said, and I grunted. The secret is out. We are sometimes jerks.

Beverly flashed a smile at my brother and me, then went back to unpacking cartons of Chinese food from a sack. Bev was my father's fourth girlfriend since Mom took off to New York, and she had stuck around the longest. In the past, Fenton and I were able to scare away Dad's girlfriends after a few weeks by performing our cold-kids routine. If Ann, Sylvia, or Maureen tried to talk to us, we'd grunt or groan or look away. If she suggested playing a board game, we'd say no thanks, we'd rather watch TV. If she then said great, let's watch TV together, Fenton or I would say no thanks, we are going to go into Fenton's room to play a board game BY OURSELVES.

Eventually it worked—Ann, Sylvia, and Maureen bailed. Fenton and I were total brats, or so they believed, and they could not see themselves spending more time with such jerky kids. The breakups were tough on Dad, and we felt bad about it, but we kept our eyes on the prize, our parents one day getting back together.

Although my brother and I believed we were doing what was best for our family, it was possible we were being selfish, hoping to have a real mom again instead of a sub. We met our match when the Ice Queen came into our lives.

The first time she visited our farm she was nice to Fenton and me. But during her second visit she took us aside while Dad was out of the room and said that she liked our father, and she wasn't going to let two "conspirators" ruin her chance at happiness.

"I know what you guys are doing, giving me the cold shoulder and the stink eye with the hope that I'll leave and never return," she said. "But that is *not* going to happen. I like your father, and it's going take more than *attitude* to get rid of me. So can we come to a truce? Work this out right here and right now?"

"No truce," I said, grabbing Fenton's arm and stomping away with him. I know it sounds like I was being a big snot, but the Ice Queen was a threat to our family, and I was unwilling to make peace with the enemy. It's been a war of words and icy looks ever since.

That day at Grandma Jean's place, even though it was midafternoon, we all sat at the dining table and ate Chinese food for dinner. Fenton and I grumbled our way through egg rolls and chicken fried rice and slimy bamboo shoots, and avoided looking at Beverly.

"Do they really eat this junk in China?" Fenton asked, examining a bamboo shoot like he suspected it was a sea creature instead of a vegetable.

Dad gave us disappointed looks but didn't say anything. Grandma Jean also didn't bust us for bad behavior, perhaps because she was talking to the Ice Queen, asking about her job as a home health nurse. "That's nice, dear," Grandma kept saying to Bev, which caused me to wonder why she was calling the Ice Queen a "dear" instead of her sons and grandkids. If there were any dears at the table, Bev was not one of them.

Then came a moment where I nearly gagged, but it had nothing to do with the spicy food. Beverly took

Dad's hand and held it on the table for everyone to see. It seemed like a declaration of ownership, as if to say, *Guess what, Fenton and Fiona, I won and you lost, and there's nothing you can do about it.* (Or maybe the Ice Queen was just expressing affection. Why was I so quick to assume that something sinister was going on whenever she was in the room?)

Anyway.

Dessert was fortune cookies. I snagged two. I cracked open the first one and saw that it contained no fortune, not even a blank piece of paper. Great, I thought, someone screwed up at the cookie factory. Lucky me!

But then I worried that the lack of fortune *was* my fortune, that the all-knowing cookie, full of ancient Chinese wisdom, was trying to tell me that things were looking bleak, but because the cookie company prohibited passing along bad fortunes so sales wouldn't plummet, the cookie decided to go with no fortune instead of a bad one.

Hoping to turn things around, I broke open my second cookie and read:

> *Whatever fortune the last cookie granted,*
> *you may double it.*

Insert psychotic laughter, followed by a feeble *help me* kind of look.

The Ice Queen couldn't stay very long after we finished dinner since she had patients to check on, mostly old folks with health problems. Those poor people, I thought, having Beverly as their nurse.

With the Ice Queen gone, Grandma Jean quickly re-depressed herself. After an hour of near-silent misery except for the loud TV, we all said good-bye to Grandma Jean, got our backs patted, and drove to the farm in Uncle Jack's Subaru.

"I hate to say this," Jack said, watching the road for cars and farm machinery, "but I was hoping that Mom would have met a man by now. It's been three years since Dad died, but to Mom I think it seems like it happened yesterday. Fresh wounds instead of healed ones. It's like she's living in a dark funk she can't get out of."

My father sighed. "I feel the same way. Heck, I'd buy a mail-order husband for Mom if I thought she'd give him the time of day. It's gotten to the point where I'm coming up with excuses to not go see her or phone her, which makes me feel even worse."

I glanced at Fenton and saw him flash a smile,

thinking, I was sure, that he had the cure for Grandma's unhappiness, and Dad's and Uncle Jack's unhappiness too, by using the light ball to bring back Grandpa Wade. But there was a huge problem. He was a dead guy, and even if the light ball brought him back he was going to be a rotting corpse, or possibly just a skeleton. Could Grandma Jean love *that*?

Some poet once wrote that love has no limits. Well, Mr. Poet, try kissing a three-year-dead zombie, and then get back to me on that limitless love thing, okay?

Neither my dad nor Uncle Jack normally drink alcohol, but when we returned to Bluebird Acres they hurried inside the house and grabbed a can of beer each from a six-pack that Dad kept on hand for visits to Grandma Jean and other emergencies.

They popped the tops and took big sips, then Dad announced that he and Jack were going for a walk, code words meaning they wanted to be alone. They left the house and walked toward the cornfield, and I imagined they were already chatting about their unhappy mother and dead father.

Fenton disappeared inside his bedroom so he could check on the undead bugs and worm, and I went outside to the porch so I could think more about our crazy plan to bring Grandpa Wade back to life, and how we would have to commit grave robbery to make it happen.

Before I could do much thinking, I glanced at the miracle tree and saw the strangest thing, a white blossom on a branch. Maple tree branches were only supposed to be able to produce two things, leaves and helicopter seeds that twist in the air on windy days and are fun to catch. They do *not* produce white blossoms.

Curious, I leaped off the porch and ran to the tree, where I saw that the blossom looked like an apple blossom, five white petals that were pinkish at the edges. I wondered if the shocked-back-to-life tree had forgotten that it was a maple tree.

And then I got a double dose of the cosmic shivers when I realized that I was looking at something *new*, something that had maybe never existed before in the *entire history of the world* and its millions of maple trees—a white blossom on a branch.

I touched it—it was very soft.

I asked it what it was doing on a maple tree—it did not answer. (If it *had* answered I would have probably dropped dead right there.)

I even named it—Edith the maple tree blossom.

But then, after a solid minute of blissful blossom wonderment, I realized that it had to go.

Yes, for the sake of science I probably should have left the blossom in place to see if it produced an apple or some other kind of fruit. But, worried that Dad and Uncle Jack would see the blossom and freak out, I plucked it.

Just as I was slipping it inside a pocket in my shorts, I heard a loud muffler. I looked to the road and saw our neighbor, Sonny Baskins, driving by in his old truck. Worry tightened my face. Did Sonny see the blossom before I plucked it? Living on a farm made it easy to forget about the neighbors, since they were pretty far away. But that didn't mean that they had forgotten about us.

"Nothing to freak out about," I told myself when Sonny Baskins and his truck were farther down the road. Boy was I wrong.

Chapter 17

A Handy Guide to
Bringing Back the Dead
(Take 2)

What you will need:

- A wheelbarrow to transport your tools and the zombie you've chosen to awaken in case he can't walk or has no legs (rats might have eaten them).
- Two shovels if there are two of you.
- Two flashlights if you plan to dig at night.
- A tire iron or other tool that can open a sealed casket.
- Gloves so your hands don't get blistered while digging.
- A baseball bat to defend yourself with in case the zombie attacks you.
- Snacks and beverages—you will be digging for a while. Note: it's unlikely that your zombie will

ask for food or water, but be prepared just in case. Second note: if he says he wants to "eat your brains," please see the above baseball bat entry.

- A scarf or a mask to cover your nose and mouth so you will not breathe in the stinky rot of death and decay, the worst odor in the universe.

- Dark clothing and Halloween face paint, or some other way to disguise yourself, in case someone sees you at the cemetery or while traveling to and from there.

- A notebook, a pen, and a camera and spare batteries, so you can document the experiment.

- A cell phone (optional) in case the thing you awaken goes on a rampage and you need help from the US Army.

- A really good story in case someone asks why you are robbing a grave.

- A second good story in case the zombie you brought back can speak and asks why you woke him up.

- A third good story in case something unexpected happens.

- Clothing and a hat for the zombie in case he is as naked as a skeleton.

- A great ball of light capable of restoring life to dead

stuff. Note: unexpected side effects are possible, so be on guard. Second note: there may only be one light ball in the world, so if it shows up in your yard one day please share it with others.

- And, most importantly, you will need tons of courage and lots of good luck.

Chapter 18

Operation Dig Up Grandpa Wade

To lessen the chance that something could go wrong, Fenton and I spent part of Saturday and Sunday planning the details of our biggest and most daring scientific experiment yet, the attempted resurrection of Grandpa Wade. But when you are talking about robbing a grave and restarting a corpse, wouldn't it pretty much be certain that *everything* would go wrong?

Two or three times I tried to talk Fenton out of digging up our grandfather, but my efforts were half-hearted. I think the reason I kept sharing my doubts and fears about Operation Dig Up Grandpa Wade (as we were calling it) was because I was hoping my brother would convince me completely—without room for a single *but what if*—that what we were doing was *scientifically important*, and to not do it would be a disservice to life and to science. Or something noble like that.

To his credit, Fenton was right about one thing: we had been given the opportunity to do something that might never have been done before, restoring life (or the next best thing) to a dead person. How could a kid possessing even a tiny wisp of curiosity say no to giving it a try?

Anyway.

We agreed to wait for a night when Dad would be at the Ice Queen's house and was planning to stay late. Our chance came that Monday, one week before Memorial Day. Coming home from school, Fenton and I found a note from Dad saying that after work he was heading to Beverly's and wouldn't be home until midnight or later.

Love you two monkeys, he wrote, and there was some kind of quality in his handwriting that told me he meant those words completely.

Our planned grave robbery was a go.

Shortly before nine o'clock, Fenton and I changed into dark clothes, then we scooped ashes from the fireplace and darkened our faces and necks.

"I feel like a criminal," he said, smearing ash on my nose—I had missed a spot.

"You *should* feel like a criminal," I said, "and so should I. Grave robbery has to be a federal crime. We could go to jail for *years*."

"But only if we are caught," he pointed out.

We gathered the supplies, and I went over the list twice to make sure we had everything. The one thing we almost forgot was the ball of light, can you believe it? But as Fenton and I neared the front door my brain kicked in, and I fetched the barrel jar and slid it into my backpack, which also held the flashlights and a tire iron, my science notebook, a pen, Dad's camera, and snacks and bottled water.

Outside, we loaded the shovels and baseball bat onto the wheelbarrow, then we talked about whether to bring Scruffy along so he could protect us from wolves and coyotes, which are not uncommon in our part of Montana since we are a few miles from the Gallatin National Forest. But we decided against it. What if someone saw us walking with a skeleton dog?

"Last chance to bail," Fenton said, and I wondered if he was hoping that I'd freak out and run inside the house and hide myself in my room so he could cancel the experiment, seeing as how it would be unfair for him to do all the work.

Instead of freaking out, I exhaled and said, "Let's do it." We walked toward the road, Fenton pushing the wheelbarrow since I was wearing the heavy backpack. The sun had set, but there were still some traces of light to the west.

"Aren't you going to say it?" he asked.

"Say what?" I said.

"The thing you always say, that you have a bad feeling about this."

"I have a bad feeling about this," I said, smiling, even though I did have a bad feeling about the experiment, and the possible implications of digging up our grandpa. Even if the cops didn't bust us for grave robbery, at some point Dad would find out what we did and completely freak out on us.

At the gravel road we began walking east toward the cemetery.

The road had no streetlights and there was no moonlight that night, so the growing dark caused a surge of fizzing fear, in part because it was hard to tell if wild animals were about to pounce on us from the shadows. Three times I talked myself into turning tail and running home, and three times I talked myself into ignoring that idea and continuing on.

"Someday," said Fenton as we passed a small farm, "we will look back on this night and the things we are about to do as the turning point in our lives, the night we went from nobodies to famous somebodies worth a million bucks apiece."

"It's also possible," I said, "that we will remember this night as the night we caused a huge screwup that could not be undone, and that we will spend the rest of our lives regretting it."

He set down the wheelbarrow and looked at me. "You're right—that could also be true. No matter what happens, good or bad, it's probably going to be something we didn't plan for."

I nodded, appreciative of the fact that Fenton had said something smart and sensible, instead of making fun of my words or showing an ugly, beleaguered face, like putting up with me was a real chore. I love it when he surprises me like that.

We were a few hundred yards from the cemetery when we saw a car or a truck coming up the road.

"Emergency plan! Emergency plan!" Fenton loudly said.

So, following our planned response to Seeing a

Car, we quickly moved ourselves and our supplies to someone's yard and froze; we were trying to look like wooden lawn ornaments should people in the car or truck see us.

As it came nearer we realized it was a car, not a truck, which scratched off our neighbor Sonny Baskins from the list of possibilities. According to the plan, if the driver stopped and asked what we were doing out by ourselves after dark, I was to run off and hide the light ball somewhere, and Fenton would tell the person that we were planning to dig up a mess of night crawlers so we could fish all summer long.

The car turned out to be an old Chevy with a hood scoop, and inside it was a young couple so caught up being lovebirds they didn't look at Fenton and me. The girl was nibbling on the guy's ear, and the guy was laughing like a hyena instead of concentrating on driving.

Ick.

We checked to make sure no more cars were coming, then Fenton returned to the road with the wheelbarrow. But I hesitated: Go right to the cemetery or left toward home?

It was then that I hooked up to the great ball of light. *It will be okay*, it said to me. And since the jar holding the light was against my back, it seemed liked those words snuck inside me and coated my organs with assurances that everything was going to be fine. Most of my worries vanished, and I felt oddly warm and confident.

None of that made sense. It was just light. I shouldn't have felt anything.

"Coming?" said Fenton, peering back at me. "Or are you going to just stand there like the world's ugliest scarecrow?"

"Coming," I said, hurrying to my brother.

Chapter 19

A Severe Case of the Cemetery Willies

The only thing creepier than a cemetery during the day is a cemetery at night. Tilted gravestones. An owl perched in a dark tree like it's watching over the dead. And all those dead people crammed together underneath the grass.

Fenton and I nervously stepped onto the cemetery grounds, then we stopped and traded sheepish looks.

"Where's Grandpa's grave?" he asked. "I kind of forgot."

"I kind of forgot too." It had been nearly a year since we had been there.

I slid off the backpack and pulled out the flashlights, then we split up and began to hunt for Grandpa Wade's grave. As I shone light on gravestones and markers, I couldn't help but read the names and the years the dead people had lived, and epitaphs like "beloved wife, mother, and daughter."

It hit me while I was reading names that each of those people had once been on this side of the dirt. They were kids like Fenton and me, and then they got older and became adults, and probably did many amazing and stupid things, and then one day they died. I felt such a deep sadness for all of them, not for the lives they had lived, but because it was game over. And there was no way for me to ask them for a quick story, a favorite memory that I could write down in my science notebook. And that felt like a huge rip-off.

An insane idea pinged through my brain: I could ask the light ball to wake up every person buried at Rolling Brook, long enough that I could record their stories and take their pictures. But the more I thought about it, the more it sounded like a bad idea. What if they didn't want to be woken up, were enjoying their rest? Or what if they left the cemetery and terrorized the citizens of Deerwood and Red Lodge? I couldn't risk it.

I went back to work and found Grandpa Wade's marker two minutes later: just his name and the years of his birth and death, no *beloved* this or *loving* that.

Not even an "R.I.P." I felt sad and weird that my dad and uncle didn't love Grandpa Wade enough to pay for an inscription. Maybe they were happy to be done with him. And now that Fenton and I were planning to bring Grandpa back for a second round of life . . . I didn't want to think about how my dad and uncle would react. It probably wasn't going to be with wild applause.

I yelled to Fenton, then we rustled up our supplies and returned to the grave.

"Ready?" he asked, holding a shovel handle against his chest.

"No, but let's do this anyway." Even though I could not pinpoint its exact location, I was certain that the no-going-back line had already been crossed.

At first we dug sideways under the grass so we could remove the sod and then replace it after we were done robbing the grave of its contents, our grandfather. Hopefully, in the light of day, no one would notice that the grave had been disturbed.

"So far so good," Fenton said, which I thought was a bit premature. We were only digging up grass. No major crimes had yet been committed.

Once the sod was removed and set aside, it was time to dig up dirt. Before we started, I dropped my shovel and pulled Dad's camera from my backpack so I could take a picture of Fenton digging the first scoop of dirt. When conducting a scientific experiment, it's important to document each step.

Fenton posed with his shovel bladed a few inches into the soil. Since it was dark I decided to use the flash, even though I was worried we would draw unwanted attention. I hoped that if someone living close to the cemetery saw the flash, they would guess that a firefly had exploded, even though it was not yet firefly season, and fireflies never exploded. My head was a little weird that night.

It took nearly an hour's worth of digging and rest breaks before we saw the casket. It was about two and a half feet below ground, which surprised me, since I thought caskets were always buried six feet deep.

"There it is," Fenton said, leaning against his shovel. "Grandpa's casket, up close and personal."

I snapped a picture of the exposed few inches of casket, then declared a third snack break. We sat near the grave and ate peanut butter crackers and drank bottled water.

"Dad is going to kill us when he finds out what we did," I said, chomping on crackers.

"Yep. And then he'll probably bury us next to

Grandpa," said Fenton. "Maybe we should dig a grave for us while we are here!"

Okay, so maybe sometimes my brother is funny.

After our break was over, we dug up dirt more carefully—we were trying to not scratch the coffin, which would have been disrespectful. As more dirt was cleared away, we slowed down a little, but it wasn't due to exhaustion. I think we were both a little fearful of what was waiting for us inside, and were trying to delay seeing it and smelling it for as long as possible.

Despite our slow pace, eventually the coffin was free of dirt, except for some crumbs. We stopped digging and looked at each other apprehensively.

"What now?" I asked, even though we had gone over the plan several times and I knew what was next.

My brother wiped dirt from his chin. "We pry open the casket, set the lightning ball inside, and let it do its thing."

"But what if it's just dust in there? And worms!"

"We try anyway. We need to know what the light ball can do."

I exhaled, then pulled the tire iron and barrel jar from my backpack and handed the tire iron to Fenton—we had agreed that he'd pry open the coffin. But as fate would have it, he didn't need to use it.

As soon as I set the jar on the ground, the light ball bounced around like it wanted out. I gazed at Fenton and he nodded, so I twisted the lid off with mixed emotions. Whenever we freed the light ball, part of me hoped that it would stick around so we could do more experimenting, and part of me wished that it would launch itself toward the clouds and we'd never see it again. And maybe we could go back to living semi-normal lives.

Free of the lid, the light ball leaped out of the jar and bounced around a little. Then, as if knowing what we wanted it to do, it shot inside the casket, passing through wood and padding without leaving a mark.

Fenton and I looked at each other and waited.

And then we waited some more. We *didn't* want anything to happen! We wanted *something* to happen.

And then we noticed that grains of dirt atop the casket were moving, just a little.

And then the dirt bits started bouncing.

And then the casket began to shake.

And then, at the very same time the owl in the tree hooted, the casket's lid flew open, smacking against the side of the grave.

Fenton shrieked. "Oh my God!

I screamed and closed my eyes. "Aah!"

And the owl *hoo-hoo*-hooted some more.

I let several seconds go by before I opened my eyes and saw the pulsing ball of light resting on Grandpa Wade's chest like it was trying to breathe life into him. Grandpa's blue suit and red tie had just about rotted away, and his skin was gray and peeling in spots, and his hair that used to be mostly brown had turned ghostly white, and his nose was messed up—all bone. But overall he looked quite a bit like Grandpa Wade, and more of a person than a skeleton. I was stunned.

Suddenly the smell of death hit us—Dumpster mixed with rotten eggs mixed with gym socks, and served with a side of newspaper soaked in cat pee. Trying hard not to gag, I grabbed two towels from the backpack and handed one to Fenton, and we covered our noses and mouths.

"Do you think the lightning ball is working?" he said through his towel, so the words were muffled. "Grandpa isn't moving, and we can't stay here all night."

I didn't say anything, mostly because I didn't want to move my mouth even a tiny bit and risk allowing odor molecules inside. But Fenton's question was valid. We had assigned a huge task to the light ball,

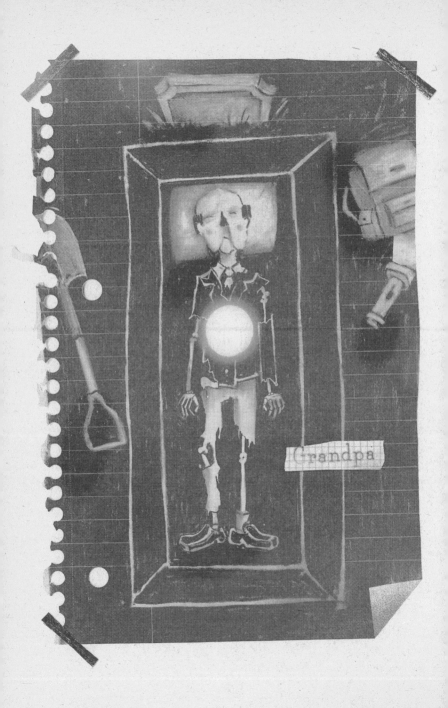

bringing a three-year-dead person back to life (or to undeath, whatever), and it seemed to be struggling to make it happen.

So we agreed to give it a half hour. If nothing changed with Grandpa Wade, we'd admit defeat, cover the coffin with dirt, and pretend none of this ever happened.

About twenty minutes passed without any sign that Grandpa Wade was about to wake up. I took a few pictures and scribbled notes in my science notebook, and at one point I dozed off while sitting near the grave. When I woke up, Fenton was talking to the light ball.

"Come on, lightning ball," he said. "You can do it. Show us your magic!"

The light kept pulsing. I wrote in my notebook:

> Maybe there isn't enough left of Grandpa Wade for the light to work with so it can do its job. Bringing back to life a hollow dog must be loads easier than bringing back a hollow person. Like rebuilding a toaster from scratch instead of a computer. Too many missing wires and rusted doohickeys to save our grandpa.

I glanced at Fenton, who was struggling to keep his eyes open. "Let's quit, okay?" I said. "Dad could be saying good night to the Ice Queen this exact minute, about to head home." I was certain that if we gave up trying to resurrect Grandpa Wade, we would never try again. We had risked too much and hoped too hard and come up empty-handed.

"Five more minutes?" he asked, and I agreed. But as it turned out we only needed another thirty seconds before the ball of light's work paid off.

Grandpa Wade's eyes suddenly shot open—they were solid gray. Fenton swore and I *ack*ed. What if we had woken up a zombie of the movie kind, and our grandpa was about to crawl out of his casket and try to strangle us so he could *eat our brains*?

"He's alive! He's alive!" said Fenton.

"I know! I know!" I said.

"Alive! I can't believe it!"

"Or sort of alive," I clarified. Grandpa Wade's chest wasn't moving, meaning that he wasn't actually alive. But he was significantly less dead.

"That's way better than being dead!" my brother said. "Right? Right?"

"Okay!" I said, trying to match Fenton's level of excitement, even though dread and worry were building up inside me. We had reached another point of no return. Those always made me feel conflicted and tied up inside.

Grandpa looked at us and his mouth moved, but no words came out. It was obvious that he was trying to say something, so we inched closer to the grave so we could hear him.

"Freddy and . . . Fiona?" he finally said, his mouth full of rotted teeth and a shriveled tongue. "So good. See you . . . again."

Seeing as how Grandpa Wade had been dead for three years, it was understandable that he had forgotten Fenton's name. Plus, he hardly knew us. As grandparents went, he was a big stinker.

"Our names are *Fenton* and Fiona," I said, goose bumps everywhere—I was talking to a *dead guy*. "But Freddy was a good guess. You got the *F* part right."

Grandpa Wade looked around in a daze. I tried to imagine what it was like, waking up inside an open casket after three years of death. And then I tried very hard to *not* imagine it, since it was a creepy thought.

"Where . . . am?" Grandpa said. He sort of whole-body sneezed, which caused a cloud of stinky death dust to drift toward Fenton and me. We covered our faces until the toxic threat had passed.

Fenton then told our grandfather that he was inside his grave at Rolling Brook Cemetery, which, I had to admit, must have been harsh news to hear. "But Fiona and I have freed you," he said boastfully.

"How . . . strange," Grandpa Wade said. He then pointed to the light ball resting on his chest and beating at a slower rate.

"That's the thing that brought you back," I said. "It's kind of a long story. I'll tell it to you while we take you home, I mean if that's okay with you. Do you want to go home with us, Grandpa?"

And then it hit me that Fenton and I, despite having the *whole weekend* to talk it over, hadn't discussed what we would do with Grandpa once he was on our farm. Where would he live? How would we keep him hidden from Dad? What if he escaped and terrorized the neighbors? Or tried to eat one of the goats? I felt like the World's Stupidest Girl. Fenton and I had planned out in detail every aspect of the first part of Operation Dig Up Grandpa Wade but had totally neglected the second part, what to do with our grandfather after we took him home.

Anyway.

Grandpa Wade had nodded in response to my invitation, causing a grating bone-against-bone sound. I sighed with worry and leaned closer and held out the barrel jar. The light ball hopped inside it.

I slipped the jar inside my backpack, then, at Fenton's suggestion, took a picture as he helped Grandpa out of his casket. My grandfather was leaving his coffin, and that launched a new set of worries. What if he tried to walk away—could we stop him? What if he collapsed into a pile of bones, but was still sort of alive—how creepy would that be? I was also worried that when Fenton and Grandpa Wade gripped hands, some of Grandpa's fingers would snap off, but it didn't happen.

"Thanks for. Help," Grandpa Wade said, upright now. "But still . . . don't know . . . what am doing here."

"No problem," my brother said. "Fiona and I really didn't have anything else to do tonight, so we thought we'd dig you up and take you home. That's why you are outside of your grave right now."

How casual sounding!

I peered at my grandfather, standing there in his rotted suit with Fenton's help and looking kind of baffled (and slightly tilted). Grandpa Wade wasn't a tall man when he was alive, but now he looked . . . shriveled: he had lost three or four inches of height, and was only a little bit taller than Fenton and me.

The rest of him looked kind of drawn in, and his head wasn't right either—definitely on the small side as heads went. To be honest he was sort of gross.

Grandpa Wade's legs buckled as soon as Fenton let go of his hand, so we quickly loaded him into the wheelbarrow, and I told him to take it easy, which might have been a stupid thing to say since he had been taking it easy for three solid years.

Needing to talk to my brother, I took his arm and led him away from Grandpa Wade. Fenton looked highly freaked out.

"What?" I said.

"I just realized that I touched a dead guy!" he said.

"And I did too!" I said, my panic enzymes kicking in big time.

We spent a minute wiping our hands on our jeans and wishing there was a running faucet nearby—and a bottle of peroxide, too. Note to readers: please add hand disinfectant or peroxide to the list of supplies you will need should you ever dig up a dead person.

"So I was thinking," I said, while Fenton tried to free himself of dead-guy germs, "that, okay, we just proved that the light ball can wake up dead people, which is totally amazing. But ... maybe we should put Grandpa back."

"Are you crazy?" Fenton said, inspecting his hands—I have no idea what he was looking for. "We didn't dig up Grandpa Wade just to dig him up; we dug him up to take him home with us."

"I know that already, but . . ." My words weren't coming together in the right order inside my head, so I gave them time to organize themselves. "Where are we going to keep Grandpa so Dad won't find him?" I finally said. "You know Dad, he'll flip out, and that will be bad for us. So I think it would be smarter to put Grandpa back in his coffin."

"Forget it," my brother said. "We are taking him home with us. I got it all figured out—he'll stay in the storm cellar until it's time to tell Dad. Jeez, Fi, you worry way too much about stuff."

"And you don't worry enough!" I fired back, knowing that I had lost *yet another* argument to my brother.

We found the shovels and returned the dirt to the grave and stomped down the sod. That took a while. As we worked, Grandpa Wade watched us but didn't say anything. I wondered what he was thinking, now that he was on this side of the grass again. What do undead people think about? As a person and a scientist, I really wanted to know.

Chapter 20

Travels with Grandpa Wade

Our grandfather weighed more than my brother and I had expected, considering how long he had been dead, so we both pushed the wheelbarrow as fast as we could, which wasn't very fast at all.

In time, Grandpa Wade became more interested in his surroundings, what little he would have been able to see. He peered at fields and dark houses and some cows near the road as we passed them.

"The . . . future," he said. "Cars fly? Col-o-nies . . . on Mars?"

"Flying cars?" said Fenton. "Jeez, Grandpa, how long do you think you've been dead? There are no flying cars yet, or colonies on Mars. That stuff is years away."

"But they are probably working on it," I said, so

Grandpa Wade wouldn't feel stupid. The old guy was recently dead. He deserved to be treated with respect.

About halfway home, Fenton and I took a break so we could rest.

While shaking blood into my arms, I started coming to my senses. There I was on the road with my brother and our undead grandpa, who we had just dug out of the ground, all of it made possible by a light ball that Fenton and I had captured during a storm one week earlier, the light capable of causing miracles that most people would not believe.

I glanced at my brother and at Grandpa and nearly laughed at the nature of our predicaments. Fenton and I were in similar boats—grave robbers, rule breakers, bad kids—but Grandpa Wade was in a different boat, the one set aside for the recently dead. I wondered what he would make of his second chance at life, and how long it would last.

"We better keep going," Fenton said, grabbing a wheelbarrow handle. I took the other handle and we pushed our grandfather toward home.

"Sing song?" Grandpa Wade said when we were farther down the road.

Fenton and I dumbly shrugged—could we say no?— then Fenton began singing "Oh, Susanna." I joined in

during the refrain. We messed up a few words, but it was a good effort. Grandpa tapped a knee to the beat, and a crooked smile had arisen on his drawn-in face. It was the strangest thing ever, but also kind of sweet, singing to our undead grandpa while he kept the beat, just past midnight.

And then came an odd thought: this was the first time Fenton and I had had a fun experience with our grandfather, the stuff of happy memories. And it took a ball of light, and lots of digging, and a miracle resurrection to make it happen. I felt cheated and lucky at the same time.

★ Chapter 21 ★

Welcome to Bluebird Acres

When we neared the farm and saw that Dad's SUV wasn't in the driveway, Fenton and I *phew*ed with relief.

"My . . . farm," Grandpa Wade said, sitting up and gazing at the land, much of it hidden by the dark night.

"Yep," I said, even though my dad now owned the property. "Dad and Fenton and I live here, and so do a bunch of animals."

"Wife?" Grandpa Wade asked.

"You mean Dad's wife?" I said. "She lives in New York City, so we hardly ever see her. Or, uh, if you mean your wife, she moved to an apartment for older folks in Red Lodge after you sort of passed away because of the car crash."

"Bad," he said, shaking his head and causing a scraping sound. I wasn't sure if he was talking about my mom moving to New York or his wife moving to Red Lodge or his drunken car crash, but the word "bad" certainly applied to all those things.

Fenton and I wheeled Grandpa Wade up the driveway and stopped near the storm cellar. "Your turn to say something," I said to my brother.

So he told Grandpa Wade that we were hoping he didn't mind living in the storm cellar for a few days until we came up with a way to tell Dad that his father was alive again. Or undead, whatever.

"Dad doesn't know anything yet, especially about us digging you up," Fenton said, scratching an arm and causing me to wonder why saying dodgy things often led to itchiness. "Fiona and I would like a little time to figure stuff out, if that works for you."

"Okay," our grandfather said, and I started to feel guilty about sticking the poor guy in a storm cellar, until it occurred to me that living inside a cellar instead of a casket could be considered a housing upgrade.

"I'm . . . alive," Grandpa Wade then said, like the realization had finally hit him.

"Pretty much!" I said, in a pumped-up way.

Fenton pulled open the cellar doors. With a mutual grunt we lifted Grandpa Wade out of the wheelbarrow and carried him down into the cellar, dropping him (gently!) on the floor when our arms gave out. My brother and I wiped our hands on our jeans, though not as frantically this time. As I turned on a flashlight so Grandpa could see his surroundings, Scruffy abandoned his rubber bone and padded up to him. I was worried that the dog saw Grandpa Wade as a pile of bones and was about to go nuts.

Instead Scruffy nuzzled against him and got back some scratches in return. "Weird," I mumbled, wondering if there was some kind of zombie law of attraction, that the fact they had both come back from death automatically made them friends.

I told my grandfather that Fenton and I would like to stay and chat, but Dad was due home any minute so we had to scram. "We'll come see you tomorrow. If you need anything . . . Uh, try to not need anything, okay?"

Grandpa blinked a few times, which I interpreted as a code of agreement, then my brother and I said good night and headed for the exit. I was on the second step, and Fenton on the third step, when Grandpa said, "Why?"

"Why . . . what? Why did Fenton and I bring you back?" I asked. Grandpa nodded.

"Because we love you, that's why." I thought for a moment. Should I tell him everything (except maybe the part where Fenton and I confess to being mad scientists)? Yes! So I added, "And, also, so you and Dad and Uncle Jack and Grandma Jean can work out your issues." There. I'd said it.

Silence for a breath or two, then Grandpa Wade said, "I . . . blew it. Big. Mess."

"I know, but maybe there's still time to fix things." What I thought but didn't say: *Don't you dare blow it this time, mister!*

Grandpa Wade said nothing more, so we continued our escape. When we were outside, my brother closed the cellar doors and leaned into them, exhausted.

"I don't believe this all really happened," he said, his voice shaking. "This is a weird dream, isn't it? Tell me it's a dream!"

"I was just thinking the same thought—no way could any of this be real," I agreed. I might have said more, but we saw headlights coming up the road: Dad, probably. Fenton pushed the wheelbarrow full of supplies to the side of the house, and we rushed inside and to our bedrooms.

In my room I shoved the backpack holding the light ball in the closet and threw a blanket over it. Dad's car was gliding up the driveway. I grabbed a towel and wiped charcoal off my face, hoping like mad that Fenton was doing the same thing. There wasn't time to get every last smear so I decided to cover my head with my bedsheet. That way I'd pass inspection when Dad looked in to make sure I was asleep.

I turned out the light and slid under the sheet, then listened as my father came inside the house. I forgot how to breathe for a moment when Dad opened the door and saw my best impersonation of a mummy. When he left to check on Fenton, I sucked in air with all the strength of a Swedish vacuum cleaner. I then sent the following psychic thought to my father: *Whatever you do, please don't look in the storm cellar.*

Mapples, anyone?

The next day at school I had a weird moment I'd like to tell you about. It was during library study hall, but instead of studying, I was trying to think of a gentle way to break the news to Dad about his father being alive again, and about Scruffy, the ball of light, everything. Plans and schemes ran through my mind, but nothing sounded plausible, or survivable. I imagined my angry dad, once he found out the truth, grounding Fenton and me well into our adult years.

At one point I looked across the library and saw Luke Stambaugh sitting at a table and gazing at me with lovestruck-buck eyes. I was debating returning lovestruck-doe eyes, when I had a big thought, basically wondering if Luke and his sister, Emily, had recently lost a favorite relative or pet, and if that was true I could—with the light ball's help—bring that person or pet back and make them happy again.

I then scanned the library, looking at all the kids and the two teachers (Mr. Embry the science guy and Miss Cash the math lady) and the librarian (Ms. Jenner, aka "Eagle Eyes"), and thinking the same thing, that if they had recently lost a pet or a relative, well, maybe I could ease their pain by bringing that person or pet back. In my mind I saw myself running around the library and making the offer to each kid and adult, and then Fenton and I would spend the rest of the week resurrecting people and dogs and cats and parakeets and whatever or whoever. And what an amazing week it would be, reuniting all these people with lost pets and relatives. Not to mention that my popularity would skyrocket.

But then I realized—total slink down in my seat kind of moment—that I couldn't do any of that. It was too soon. Fenton and I didn't know yet what the light ball was fully capable of, and how restored people and animals would behave not just a day or a week later, but three months down the road. What if the undead eventually turned violent and needed to be "put down" for the greater good?

So, for that reason, and other reasons, including that our farm might get invaded by thousands of strangers once the word got out, I could not make any offers of restoration of dead pets and people. Even though they had no knowledge of my thoughts or the light ball, it seemed like I had just let down Luke and the rest of the kids and adults at the library. I felt pretty cruddy the rest of the day.

When Fenton and I stepped off the school bus that afternoon, intent on checking on Grandpa, we quickly saw that there was a crisis to deal with: dozens of apple blossoms, and small green apples, had appeared on the maple tree while we were gone. Never mind that apples usually appear *after* the blossoms have vanished. This was a maple tree!

"Crud!" I said, running to the tree, Fenton not far behind. "We need to get rid of the apples before Dad comes home."

I dashed to the outbuilding, found a wicker basket that we used to collect fruit and veggies and eggs, and returned to the maple tree. Fenton was about to bite into a tiny apple.

"Don't eat that!" I yelled. "It could be poison."

He tossed the apple into the basket. "Really?"

"I'm not sure, but we better be careful. Better safe than sorry, right?"

"I have a better way to say it. Better safe than dead."

As fast as we could, we pulled the apples and blossoms from the tree and dropped them into the basket. While we worked, I looked over at the Baskins property and saw Sonny in his front yard, standing near some rosebushes. He saw me and weirdly saluted, so I saluted back and watched him go inside his house.

"Trouble," I said to Fenton. "I think Mr. Baskins saw the apple tree. I mean the maple tree with apples. Whatever!"

My brother nodded. "In that case we better kill Sonny Baskins. Feed him poison apples until his big fat belly explodes. Ka-boom!"

Not!

"Here's what I think. We better tell Dad everything as soon as he gets home," I said. "Before Sonny Baskins or someone else beats us to it."

Fenton looked worried, but he helped me yank apples off the tree. And I had one of those this-is-my-weird-life moments—you know, when you're doing something freaky, like, say, pulling apples from a maple tree and treating it like it was a normal thing. I guess that was my way of dealing with the craziness, dressing giant-sized moments in regular-sized clothes so they were easier to deal with.

After we had plucked the apples and blossoms, we took the basket into the storm cellar so Dad wouldn't see them. Grandpa Wade was on the floor with Scruffy. The dog gnawed on the rubber bone.

Grandpa said, "Look at . . . me, kids," and shakily stood up. He took a few steps, wobbled, and collapsed to the floor, but seemed proud of himself.

"You are doing great," I said. "Keep practicing and soon you will be a champion walker." I wondered if he was hungry. Do the undead get hungry?

My brother then had a great idea: we would whittle a walking stick for Grandpa Wade to help him get around better. All we needed to get started was a fallen branch, and there were lots of those on our farm. We told Grandpa we'd have the walking stick ready for him in an hour.

He smiled and said thanks, and I remembered that

the pasty-looking guy over there was my grandfather. So maybe he was ready to pass on some grandfatherly advice?

"Hey, Grandpa?" I said. "Dad'll be home soon, and Fenton and I are going to tell him about you, Scruffy, and the ball of light. You know him as well as we do, maybe better. Any advice on how we might tell the story and not cause him to blow a circuit?"

Grandpa Wade thought for a moment. "Get drunk?"

I frowned. It didn't really matter whether Grandpa Wade was suggesting that Fenton and I get drunk, or that we get our father drunk before we told the story. Alcohol had ruined our grandfather's life and caused his death—he crashed his car into a tree while drunk. And now he had the gall to suggest it as a remedy? I can't tell you how ticked off I was feeling.

Fenton and I left the cellar, yours truly wondering if we had royally screwed up by digging up Grandpa Wade, that lifelong lover of booze. And, apparently, a deathlong lover of booze too.

* Chapter 23 *

Extreme Father Issues

In the living room, Fenton and I spent a half hour rehearsing what we were going to say to our dad. We agreed that I would do most of the talking. I'm better than Fenton at adding sugar and chocolate sprinkles to difficult words, making them tastier and easier to digest.

At five o'clock we heard our dad's car crunching up the driveway. My brother and I traded worried looks, then we went to the picture window and watched as Dad climbed out of his SUV, gazed fondly at the miracle tree, and walked to the house.

"My life just flashed before my eyes," Fenton said.

"I think that was my life you saw flashing by," I said.

When Dad came inside, Fenton and I hugged and kissed him, and tried to give the impression that we were the most loving children to ever walk the earth. At one point Dad asked how school went, but I just mumbled something. It was like my mind was so full of thoughts and worries and rehearsed words it was having trouble accessing memory modules, including about how school went.

We followed Dad into the kitchen so he could snag a bottle of iced tea from the fridge, and then into the living room so he could check the mail. "Is something going on with you two?" he asked, flipping through bills and junk mail.

Fenton zapped me with a *say something* look, so I, the spokesperson for Disaster Enterprises Incorporated, started talking.

"Um, Dad?" I said. "There's something Fenton and I need to tell you—nothing weird, or anything, just some stuff. But maybe you should sit down before we start."

"I'm fine standing—I was kneeling all day at work," he said. "As it turns out, I have something important to say to you guys, too. But why don't you go first. I haven't figured out how I want to say it yet."

"That's okay," I said, smiling. "You should go first. Take all the time you need!"

Dad nodded, and while he was searching for the right words to say, I heard someone step onto the front porch.

I was worried it was Sonny Baskins, planning to ask Dad about the apples he had seen growing on the maple tree, and then, once the story fell out of our mouths, my brother and I would be so deep in doo-doo we would need to take a dozen showers to get rid of the stink.

Instead, the door opened and Grandpa Wade entered, wearing his funeral suit and holding a flash-light. "Need . . . batteries," he said. He stepped toward the kitchen, then dropped to the floor and decided to crawl instead.

So much for careful planning!

Dad pointed to his dead father and looked like he was trying to say something, but no words came out. Suddenly his eyes rolled back, and before I could try

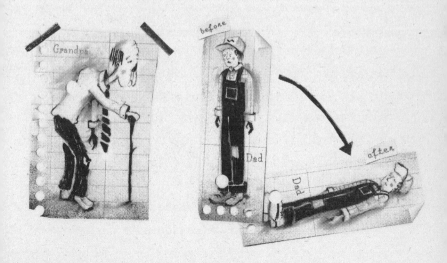

to catch him he fainted and collapsed to the carpet, just exactly like in the movies.

"Not how I saw it playing out," Fenton said, gazing at our unconscious father.

"No duh," was my brilliant response.

Grandpa Wade had left the storm cellar doors open, so Scruffy trotted in next. He went up to Dad and looked like he wanted to awaken him by licking his face, but he couldn't since he no longer had a tongue. But sometimes it's the thought that counts, right?

Chapter 21

Faint of Heart

I had no idea that people living in the real world could faint due to a sudden shock. I thought it was something that only happened in books and movies, and it was always a woman or a girl doing the fainting. Kind of sexist, if you ask me. Men and boys deal with stuff, while women and girls knock themselves out.

In real life, our dad had truly fainted and was still unconscious thirty seconds later. So I ran for a washcloth, soaked it with cold water, and returned to my father and dabbed his face with it.

He opened his eyes and looked at me, and then he sat up and rubbed at the back of his head. "What happened?" he asked groggily, checking for bumps.

"You had a bit of a fright," I said, dabbing his face some more.

"That's right," he said, looking off into the distance. "I thought I saw my dead father walking through the front door, like he'd come back from the grave. A hallucination, obviously."

Fenton cleared his throat, then pointed to the couch where Grandpa Wade sat in tattered clothes and thin skin, Scruffy the skeleton dog at his feet.

Dad gaped at his father and at Scruffy, and looked like he was trying to say something, but his mouth was only capable of forming drool, not sentences. His eyes rolled back, but this time I caught him before he slammed to the floor. I gently set his head on the carpet.

"I'm going for ice," Fenton said, scurrying into the kitchen. I turned to Grandpa Wade and asked if he and Scruffy could return to the storm cellar, that the shock of seeing them was too much for Dad to handle all at once, but we'd call them when he was ready to deal with it.

Grandpa Wade nodded and made a strange request: Could he borrow a few books in case he was going to be in the cellar awhile? I had never thought of my grandfather as a reader, but I ran into the den and pulled books by Charles Dickens and Ernest Hemingway off the shelves and handed them to Grandpa. He and Scruffy left, and I said a silent plea to the universe that no one driving by on the road saw them before they got inside the cellar.

Fenton poured several ice cubes down Dad's shirt, which caused him to instantly awaken and sit up.

"Okay, what's going on here?" he said, shaking ice out from under his shirt and scrunching up his face. "Because a moment ago I was seeing things that could not possibly be there. Some kind of brain glitch, I guess. I better schedule an appointment with Dr. Forrest, get an exam from head to toe."

"Actually, Dad," I said, "the things you think you saw you did see. It's kind of a funny story."

"Almost a hilarious story!" Fenton said. I guess he was trying to be helpful by diluting some of the weirdness. It didn't work.

"What are you guys talking about?" Dad asked. He was starting to get some color back.

I handed the cold rag to my father and suggested that he keep dabbing his face with it. Then I began telling him, shakily and not always in the right order, about the storm, and the light ball, and the experiments Fenton and I conducted, and about digging up Scruffy and Grandpa Wade for the sake of science and our family. Since then, I said, Grandpa Wade and Scruffy have been living in the storm cellar.

"It's sort of like Grandpa Wade and Scruffy are alive, but it's more like they are, well, undead," I said. "Scruffy, it turns out, is pretty much hollow, and I'm not sure what's going on inside Grandpa. Probably not much." Fenton smiled after I finished, which was his entire contribution to my ten-minute confession.

Dad went pale. "I think I'm going to be sick."

"Perfectly understandable," I said, signaling Fenton to get a bucket in case Dad needed to retch. "It had to be shocking, seeing your dad again. Fenton and I are also freaking out, but we are a bit more used to it, I guess."

"So this isn't just an elaborate prank?" Dad said, patting his face with the rag. "Ha-ha. You got me, kids!"

"Sorry, Dad," I said. Fenton and I had done a lousy job when it came to planning ahead for the day we'd have to tell everything to Dad.

I fetched my science notebook and the ball of light, and when I returned Dad was sitting on the couch next to Fenton, sipping an iced tea Fenton must have brought him. My brother crossed his eyes at me, a look I read as saying, *At least Dad hasn't murdered us.* True, but it was early.

I sat on the other side of Dad and showed him my notebook, then I handed the barrel jar to him. He looked at the pulsing light like he was in the presence of something holy. It was a strange but awesome sight, seeing the light ball shine on my father's face.

"So this is the troublemaker," he said, touching the jar in different places like he was expecting heat, not just light. "You really think it's a lightning ball?"

"Fenton does," I said. "But I think it's something different, something more rare, that just happened to land in our yard during the storm."

Dad looked at the light for another half minute, then handed the jar to me and began patting his forehead with the rag.

"Things like this don't happen in real life," he said, kind of weakly. "Please, one of you tell me that we are starring in a TV show like *Candid Camera*, and that none of this is real."

"That's what I was thinking too," I said, "that I somehow got stuck inside a novel about a light ball that can do miraculous things. But it's real."

"Even more real than real life," Fenton added. At first I thought it was a dumb remark, but then I realized it might have been super deep. Like say you are living in a black-and-white world, then suddenly something comes along and it changes into a world of a million colors. Same world, but more enhanced. Does that make any sense?

Dad wanted to see the resurrected bugs and worm, so my brother helped him stand up, then we led him into Fenton's room. The bugs still looked like bugs, but the worm had grown longer and plumper, and eight tiny feet had sprouted from its sides, which allowed it to scamper inside the dresser drawer millipede style.

"These bugs, they were dead before you treated them with the light ball?" Dad asked.

"As dead as doornails," Fenton said. "But two minutes inside the jar and they were good to go."

Dad picked up the worm and examined it, focusing on the tiny pink feet.

"Sometimes the ball of light causes unexpected side effects," I said, wondering why I was so nervous.

My dad put the worm back and wiped his hands on his pants. I asked if he was ready to go see Grandpa and Scruffy, and the basket of maple apples that Fenton and I had picked. "Maybe later," he said. "I need to do some serious thinking first."

He shuffled out of the room, down the hall, and toward the front door, saying he would be back in an hour. Fenton then remembered what our dad had said when he came home, that there was something important he wanted to tell us. He called out to Dad, asking what it was as we followed him into the living room.

"That's right," Dad said, turning toward us. "I wanted to tell you that Beverly has agreed to marry me, and that we are planning for an August wedding." He froze, then added, "Of course now that my family includes an undead father-in-law and a dog that's a skeleton . . ." He left that sentence hanging in midair.

Outside, Dad crawled inside his car and headed up the driveway. At the road he turned right without using the blinker. He *always* used the blinker. He was in no shape to be driving, but he was already on the road, so there was no way to stop him. My worries were so many they piled on top of each other.

"Sorry, Dad," I said, though of course he didn't hear me. I looked at Fenton as he dropped down on the couch. "We screwed up," I said. "Big time."

"I know," he said. "But . . ."

"There are no 'buts' involved," I said. "It's a total screwup, and nothing you say will lessen it or make it sound any better than what it is, a screwup of the highest order."

My brother nodded and covered his face with his hands. And I had no idea what to do with myself, or how to fix things with Dad. Sometimes being on this side of the point-of-no-return line is a terrible thing.

Chapter 25

The Bookworm Zombie

I wish I could tell you that Dad came home a little bit later and hugged and kissed Fenton and me and said that, even though we were rotten kids, he loved us to the end of the galaxy and back. And then he hurried down to the storm cellar, and he and Grandpa Wade spent the rest of the night talking out their issues.

What really happened was that Dad did not return until after eleven, and his glassy eyes and pickling-juice odor told Fenton and me that he had been to one of the bars in Red Lodge.

"Welcome home," my brother and I said at the same time, but Dad didn't answer us. Instead he sat us on the couch and announced the punishment for our crimes, including leaving home after dark and grave robbery: an entire month without TV, no computer use except for school work, and until further notice our weekly allowances were going to be donated to charity.

"You two are on short leashes," he said. "Any further violations of trust will be treated more severely."

Violations of trust. Those three words stabbed at me, caused a kind of internal bleeding. We accepted our punishment without protest, thankful that it wasn't worse.

Dad then told me to hand over the light ball—he was going to be in charge of it from now on. I had returned the jar to my closet, so I brought it to him.

"You're . . . not going to get rid of it, are you?" asked Fenton, kind of sheepishly. "I'm just wondering, because it's possible that the lightning might come in handy in the future if something bad happens."

"I haven't decided what I'm going to do," Dad said. "But you are in no position to make requests, young man."

He told us to brush our teeth and get to bed, and to absolutely *not* tell anyone at school about our experiments. "Some people out there would be willing to do anything to get their hands on the lightning ball if they knew what it can do. We need to keep the secret—and the light—under lock and key. Got it?"

"Got it," Fenton said, and I nodded and tried to think of just the right words to say to my dad, but nothing was coming together inside my head.

I went into the bathroom and brushed my teeth, feeling pretty icky inside. Fenton and I had some work to do when it came to restoring Dad's faith in us. Plus, we had Grandpa Wade in the cellar; how long could he just stay there? And then there was the Ice Queen to deal with—Ice Stepmom? Ugh! The world was squeezing in on all sides.

As the days passed, Dad showed no interest in talking to Grandpa Wade, or even acknowledging that he was living in the storm cellar. The one thing he did do right away was donate some clothes to his father; they were too big for Grandpa, but he didn't complain. That was about it. Dad would wake up and eat breakfast and go to work and come home, and sometimes go see the Ice Queen for a few hours. Not one word about Grandpa, or even about Scruffy, a dog he used to be fond of, and he showed no interest in the miracle tree. It was like he was pretending that none of it had ever happened.

Fenton and I, on the other hand, were getting used to having Grandpa Wade living with us, were even starting to like it. We'd visit with him and Scruffy before and after school, and sometimes after dinner. We had no idea how long Grandpa would be with us, and we didn't want to waste the chance to get to know him better.

One thing I found funny, and cool, was that Grandpa Wade had become a total bookworm. He quickly read through Dad's collection of novels, so I lent some of my books to him, including my Harry Potter first editions—not exactly Dickens or Hemingway, I know. I thought the thick Harry Potter books would slow him down, but I was wrong—he read the first novel in one day.

"Tell me," he asked one afternoon, "do Ron'n . . . Her-mione. Boy-friend—girl-friend? Thought I . . . picked up. Vibe."

"Sorry, Grandpa," I said. "You'll have to read the complete series to find out what happens to them." Grandpa Wade gave me a thanks-for-nothing look and went back to reading the second Harry Potter book.

Fenton and I had put ourselves in charge of "grandpa maintenance," which involved reminding him to change his clothes each day, and when dirty clothes piled up we washed and dried them. Normally we hated washing and drying clothes, but this felt like something different, like we were taking care of an elderly relative who could not take care of himself.

Every day or two after dark, Fenton and I would take Grandpa Wade outside and hose him down. He didn't seem to mind the shower, though Fenton and I had to be careful not to blast the water too hard, or a layer of skin or clumps of hair would fly off. Yes, it was strange, hosing down my undead grandfather while he stood there in his underwear, but I simply added it to the long list of freaky things I had seen and done since the day of the storm. When you are living in a weird world, it's the normal stuff that stands out, not the weird stuff.

One night when my brother and I were leading a soaked Grandpa Wade, clomping along with the help of his walking stick, back to the storm cellar, he peered inside the house and saw my dad in his chair, reading a science-fiction novel.

"Some day," Grandpa Wade said. "He say . . . hi? To me?"

"I hope so, Grandpa," I said, not at all sure if it would ever happen. I looked at Grandpa's gray eyes and saw a ton of hurt in them. Later that night I wrote this in my science notebook: *you don't have to be alive to feel pain*.

Chapter 26

The 1990 Montana State Fair

The first Saturday in June, Dad decided to cook hamburgers on the grill. If the ball of light had not come into our lives, he probably would have invited Beverly and Grandma Jean to spend the afternoon on the farm. But lately no one was visiting us. We had to be careful to not let anyone find out about the light ball and what Fenton and I had done with it, Dad often reminded us, judgment heavy in his eyes.

I hadn't seen the light ball since Dad had taken it, but I was sure it was somewhere close. Sometimes I'd have a weird connection thing happen with the light ball where it seemed like it was shining on me and saying that everything was going to be okay, which I found hard to believe. The light had much more confidence that Dad would work things out with Grandpa Wade than I did.

Other times, a tingling sensation in my stomach reminded me that the great ball of light was somewhere close. That was on top of the dull stomachache I'd had ever since Dad had gotten mad at Fenton and me.

Weighed down by the feeling that things needed to change or none of us would ever be happy again, I decided I had to say something to Dad about his father. So, while Fenton was putting together a toy rocket on the porch, I went in back and found Dad standing over the grill, watching charcoal gray over.

"How's the fire going?" I asked, slipping my hands into the back pockets of my shorts. I felt oddly shy, like I was talking to a stranger instead of to my father.

"It should be ready in twenty minutes," said the leading expert on barbecues. Seriously, when it comes to barbecues my dad really knows his stuff.

I kicked at some grass. "So I was thinking that instead of three chairs I could set out a fourth one, for Grandpa. It would be good for him to get some sunshine and fresh air." I avoided Dad's eyes.

"Why would a man without working lungs need fresh air and sunshine?" he asked, using tongs to move around coals.

I was ready with an answer. "Everyone likes fresh air and sunshine, no matter how alive they are. Plus, Grandpa Wade might enjoy spending time with all of us, not just Fenton and me."

Dad huffed and moved more coals but didn't say anything.

"Is that a yes?" I asked, one or two hopeful molecules bouncing around inside of me.

"It's a do-whatever-you-are-going-to-do," he said, dismantling the hill of briquettes he had just built.

I suppressed a yip, then ran and gave Fenton the good news, that Dad had agreed to be in the same vicinity as Grandpa Wade. My brother smiled, but quickly pointed out a problem: It was daylight, so how were we going to take Grandpa to the backyard without being seen by neighbors or by someone driving by on the road? Once we were in back we would be safe, since the only unblocked view was from the farm behind us, which had been vacant for a year. But first we had to get there.

Fenton and I put our thinkers together and decided we would roll up Grandpa Wade in a blanket and carry him in back, and since we didn't have to worry about Grandpa passing out due to lack of oxygen we wouldn't have to rush it.

Two minutes later, blanket in hand, we were explaining our idea to Grandpa Wade.

"You sure . . . okay?" he said, worried. "Wouldn't . . . want. Step on. Toes."

"It will be fine," I said. "Now lie down on the blanket so we can roll you up."

As Fenton and I wrapped him up, I had the sensation that I was behaving like a murderer who had enlisted her brother in a scheme to hide the body from the cops.

We lifted Grandpa up and heaved him to the doors. Scruffy tried to follow us, but my brother said, "Stay!" and for once the dog obeyed. The odds of us being able to sneak two undead creatures into the backyard were not as good as sneaking one, and Grandpa Wade was the priority.

With a lot of teeth-gritting and huffing and puffing, we finally got our grandfather into the backyard, a safe distance from the grill Dad was hovering over like each coal needed his complete attention. I was going to say a funny "ta-da" as we finished unwrapping Grandpa, but then I saw that he was lying motionless, his eyes closed. Oh my God, did we accidentally kill him? Then another thought came next: Could you kill someone who wasn't exactly alive to start with?

Before panic fully set in, Grandpa Wade opened his eyes and looked around like he wasn't sure where he was. Fenton and I helped him into a chair, and I asked if he needed anything. He didn't immediately answer, but he did cough up a small bone.

"Some . . . glue?" Grandpa finally said, making a joke. Fenton and I smiled. Dad was building a new briquette pyramid, taller this time. But he hadn't found an excuse to leave, which I took as a positive sign.

For a few minutes we all just sat there like a family of mutes. Then Dad glanced at Grandpa Wade and said, "So how's it going in the cellar?"

"Can't . . . complain," Grandpa said. "Better than— last place. Was kind of . . . dark, and cramped. Couldn't open. Door."

My brother and I chuckled, and Dad smiled for about two seconds. I hoped that he and Grandpa were going to have a serious conversation about their problems, or at least talk about the weather, the farm, the stock market, something or anything. But I was worried it would never happen if it was left up to them.

So I tried to nudge them a little. "Hey, Grandpa. When Dad and Uncle Jack were kids, did you guys have lots of barbecues?"

"Yes," he said. "Mostly . . . hot dogs. Had some. Lean years."

"I'm surprised you can remember any of the barbecues we had," Dad said, pressing a spatula hard against a burger so the fat would burn up. "You were smashed during nearly all of them."

"I guess . . . that's fair," Grandpa Wade said, dropping his head—I thought I heard something pop.

Okay. So this was going badly.

I looked to Fenton for some help, but he was busy aiming a finger gun at two Canadian geese flapping across the sky, and probably saying "kerpow" inside his dark head. A fresh idea then struck me.

"I know, let's play a game where everyone says one of their favorite memories," I said. "Nothing sad or bad or weird, just the happy stuff. The oldest person can go first. Hey, Grandpa, that's you!"

Grandpa Wade gave me a growly look, but then, somewhere deep inside his dusty bones, he found this.

"Montana . . . State Fair. 1990—I think. Great Falls. Took family. Spent . . . whole day. Midway rides . . . games. Tossed baseball. Won—stuffed bear. Greasy food. Tractor . . . pull. Pony rides—for kids. Drove home late. Jack 'n' your . . . father. Fell asleep—in back. Carried them . . . inside. Put to bed. Smiles . . .

on faces. Good day." He rubbed his right eye like he was expecting tears, but there weren't any. The dead are pretty dry.

"Thanks, Grandpa," I said. "So, Dad, what do you remember about the state fair?"

"I remember all the years we *didn't* go to the fair," he said, attacking another burger with the spatula, "because your grandfather had lost his license due to drunken driving, or he and mom were fighting, or for other stupid reasons."

"Okay," I said, "but what do you remember about the state fair you did go to, the one in 1990? Did they have a Ferris wheel? Did you and Jack stuff yourselves with funnel cakes and cotton candy like Fenton and I like to do?"

Dad softened a little. "Sure, we had fun at the fair. We ate lots of junk food and went on most of the rides. When we got off of a ride called the Cyclone, your uncle threw up on the shoes of an older couple, which they did not appreciate, though we thought it was hilarious. Later, at the petting zoo, Jack asked the guy running it why they didn't have any lions or tigers or bears to pet. 'This is a zoo, isn't it?' he said. 'So where are the cool animals?' Jack could be a real cutup."

"And then you guys fell asleep on the way home," I

said, hoping for a little more. "And your dad carried you inside and tucked you in your beds."

"I don't remember that part," Dad said flatly. "But it sounds like something that could have happened." He wiggled his nose like he was fighting a sniffle.

We were back to silence, but that was okay. It seemed like my father had just done something brave by sharing a happy memory in front of his father. I decided to not share my own happy memory, or bug Fenton for one, so as to not take away from what I thought might be, well, a major breakthrough.

When the burgers were ready, Dad, Fenton, and I applied fixings and wolfed them down, while Grandpa watched us with envy. Apparently the undead can crave barbecued meat, even though they don't eat or drink. Who knew!

I was glad that Dad was willing to eat his hamburger and waffle chips with his father nearby, but the grace period didn't last long. As soon as Dad finished eating, he said he was due at Beverly's house in Red Lodge and was running late. He hugged Fenton and me and left.

Grandpa Wade's face filled up with sadness.

"Don't worry," I said encouragingly. "Things will

get better with Dad soon, he just needs some time. But I think we made progress today with the state fair stories, don't you?"

"Apprec-i-ate efforts," he said. "Don't . . . deserve it. I was. Bad dad."

"That's true," Fenton said, rubbing away some catsup near his mouth. "And you weren't exactly the world's greatest grandfather, either."

I blasted him with fiery eyes, then told Grandpa that the important thing was that he was trying to make things right and be a better guy. "So instead of think-ing of yourself as a bad dad, maybe it would be better to think of yourself as a good dad who did some bad and foolish things, like drinking booze *way* too often."

"Thanks . . . Fiona," he said, but it didn't look like he felt one bit better about himself. Platitudes don't always change attitudes, I guess.

As I gathered the dinner plates and set them on the tray of condiments that flies were circling, my grand-father asked how his wife, Jean, was doing.

"She's fine," I lied. "It's really busy over at her apartment complex. They play bingo like four times each week."

That was the seventh or eighth time Grandpa Wade had asked about his wife, and each time I was uncomfortable. One of the reasons we dug up our grandfather was so he could reunite with Grandma Jean, and they would be as happy as well-fed cats.

But I was starting to wonder whether Grandpa Wade would ever see his wife again. He was still looking corpselike—I wasn't so sure my grandmother would want anything to do with him. Yeah, yeah, yeah, I *know* that looks are less important than how a person is on the inside, but Grandpa Wade didn't have much going on in his insides. So how was he going to win back Grandma Jean's love?

Chapter 27

Spiraling Rocket, Mortal Mouse

Fenton and I stayed outside with Grandpa Wade for a little while, not really talking about anything, but we were pretty jazzed that we had a grandfather we could hang out with whenever we wanted to—something new. But then Grandpa said he wanted to go do some reading in the storm cellar.

"Might still . . . be alive," he said, "if I had. Loved—books. During my . . . first life. Been too busy reading. To drink."

I thought he was right, but I have to admit I was also a tiny bit upset that he was ditching my brother and me so he could read a book. At least we had lost to a worthy opponent.

We rolled Grandpa up in the blanket and carried

him back to the cellar. I told him we would stop by later to say good night before we went to bed. I was about to leave, when Fenton spat out a question we'd both been wondering about but hadn't dared to ask.

"So, what was it like being dead?"

Grandpa Wade was sitting on the blanket, so Fenton and I dropped down near him. We figured his answer might take a while, and it did. Later I wrote down what he said in my science notebook. I'll give you the cleaner version with missing words filled in so it will be easier to read.

GRANDPA: It was very strange. I remember being surrounded by darkness, like there was no light anywhere in the world. Suddenly there was a bright flash, and I found myself walking down a tunnel toward a golden light that had a beat to it, like a heart. There were several shadowy figures up ahead, and as I moved closer I realized that they were my parents, two aunts and my uncle George, and my cousin Ronald, who had been killed in the Vietnam War. I ran to them, and it felt like I was going home.

FENTON: Wow—cool. Just like in the movies, with the tunnel of light and the dead relatives.

GRANDPA: If you say so, Freddy [he meant Fenton] . . . Suddenly, the light went away and I was standing outside hundreds of tall white pillars that seemed to go on forever in both directions. There was a small amount of space between the pillars, but not enough that I could pass through them. I tried to climb one of them, but it was made out of marble, or something just as slippery, and I didn't get anywhere. It seemed like my goal was to somehow get past the pillars, but I couldn't figure out how to do that. It was frustrating!

FENTON: Could you have dug under the pillars like a dog would?

GRANDPA: I never thought of that. But I did see a stone bench, so I sat down and waited for someone to come along and tell me what the pillars were all about, and how to get past them.

FIONA: Do you think heaven was on the other side of the pillars? Did you see any angels, or like some dead people, their souls?

GRANDPA: No, it was just me. Maybe it was heaven on the other side, but I wasn't sure. At least I didn't see any flames or hear anyone screaming, so that was good.

FIONA: How long did you sit on the bench, Grandpa?

GRANDPA: Until everything suddenly went dark again, and then I was drawn to a different kind of light. And when I opened my eyes I saw you and Freddy—

FIONA: I think you mean Fenton!

GRANDPA: Right. I saw you and Freddy crouched over my grave. And here I am, back in the world.

FIONA: So you waited on the bench for three years?

GRANDPA: I guess I did, but it didn't seem that long. A day or two at most.

FIONA and FENTON: Wow!

GRANDPA: Yeah! Wow!

Finished with the story, Grandpa Wade let out a long puff of stale air that caused Fenton to pinch up his nose. Even though it was obvious that Grandpa wanted to be left alone so he could do some reading, we stuck around a little while longer. Not to be annoying, I don't think, but because our grandfather had just shared something kind of deep and important with us for the *first time ever*. So I guess we wanted to hang out with him for a little bit, just like kids with living grandpas get to do.

Later, while Fenton finished piecing together his rocket, I thought about what my grandfather had told us.

I wondered if the reason Grandpa Wade had not been allowed into the afterlife was because someone in heaven, a supervisor or an angel, knew that one day a ball of light would appear on our farm, and that Fenton and I would use it to bring back our grandfather, but the only way it could happen was if Grandpa Wade hadn't fully crossed over. I know it sounds strange, that maybe some of the big events in our lives (and deaths?) are planned out in advance, but it could be true. Ever since the great ball of light appeared, I have come to believe that the world I thought I knew I barely know at all. It's so much more whacked than I had realized!

I got a dose of the big-idea shivers, thinking those thoughts, and was happy for the distraction when Fenton announced that the rocket—a Stratus 790 said a sticker—was ready for its inaugural flight. I joined him in the front yard, where he stuck the metal guiding rod into the ground and made sure the engine was properly packed. He lit the igniter plug and jumped back, and we watched the rocket blast into the air, leaving behind a cloud of white smoke.

It flew straight for a while, but then it curved toward the cornfield. We lost sight of it, so we ran toward the field, hoping we could find it wherever it had landed. Fenton had three engines left and was planning at least three more flights.

We walked through rows of corn, most of it only about eight inches tall. After five minutes of searching, my brother found the rocket near the edge of the field. It had a burn mark on its bottom half, and he was worried that he might have wasted his money on a rocket that was only good for one flight.

"Sixteen dollars and seventy-two cents down the drain," he said, scowling.

"'Up in smoke' might be a better way to put it," I said. Yeah I know, corny. It sounded more clever before it came out of my mouth.

As we walked through the cornfield toward the house, I saw something that at first frightened me slightly, and then fully, when I realized what it was: a dead field mouse, the one Fenton had experimented on and brought back to life, and then I set free due to its disturbing jitters and jumps. Its lack of guts gave it away.

"This could be bad," I said, pointing to the mouse. Was the dead mouse proof that the gift of life provided by the light ball was a short-term deal? It was one thing to have a mouse reach its expiration date, and another thing altogether if it was your dog or grandpa that stopped ticking.

Fenton picked up the mouse and examined it. "No bite marks or other evidence that it was killed by an animal. Huh. I guess it just stopped."

"But what if this means that Grandpa Wade and Scruffy will one day just stop?" I said. "And if that's true, how do we tell Grandpa that he might soon . . . I don't want to say it."

Worry lines wrinkled up Fenton's forehead. "To the lab," he cried, running to the house, clutching the dead mouse. I followed, breathlessly.

Chapter 28

"Ten thousand more volts!" said Dr. Frankenstein.

Inside Fenton's room we checked on the bugs and worm living in the dresser drawer. I thought they looked fine, but then Fenton noticed that the regenerated leg on the one beetle had fallen off and had not been replaced by a new one.

"More bad news," he said, exhaling. "Okay, you should document all of this in your science notebook so future generations will be warned that what the lightning ball does might not last very long."

I fetched my notebook and Dad's camera and did some more documenting, including taping the lost beetle leg onto a sheet of lined paper with Scotch tape. A question popped into my head: If people were asked if they wanted to be brought back after they died, but they could only stick around for a few weeks, would they want to do that or be left alone? I guessed that most people would want some bonus time, but not all of them would.

Maybe the better thought was how Grandpa Wade would have answered that question if we had somehow been able to ask it while he was still alive. But now . . . I couldn't imagine having to say good-bye to him in a week or a month if the light's gift wore off, especially now that he was *sometimes* behaving like a proper grandfather. Plus, he hadn't fixed things yet with Dad. He really needed to stick around awhile.

Fenton and I agreed to release the bugs and worm on the farm, just in case their little motors were winding down. It was like compassionate prison release, which I saw once on TV, where they let dying bad guys go so they can run around in the sun one last time before popping off. (Or rob another bank while there's time—it doesn't always go as planned.)

But first we decided to break Dad's rule that we were not allowed to play with the light ball unless he gave the okay. We guessed that the barrel jar was inside Dad's room, but we guessed wrong. After twenty minutes of searching I found it in the attic, inside a box marked XMAS DECORATIONS, and that was only because I sensed it pulsing in there. Clutching the jar to my chest, I felt like I was reuniting with a friend.

Insert warm, touchy-feely moment.

I took the jar to Fenton's room, where he dropped the dead mouse inside it and twisted the lid. We crossed our fingers and waited. We even left for a minute to grab beverages from the fridge, then returned and waited some more.

But nothing happened to the mouse, not a tremble or a whisker wiggle. It seemed like the ball of light was trying hard to do its magic, but it wouldn't take. In some ways that was a relief—neither of us wanted to deal with a gutted mouse hopping around again—but mostly it was a disappointment, since it could mean that if Grandpa Wade and Scruffy died a second time, there would be no bringing them back.

"Why do you suppose the light only works once?" my brother asked, dispirited.

"No idea," I said, trying, and failing, to work out that question in my head.

After we released the bugs and mutant worm near the barn and wished them well, we buried the dead mouse in the pet graveyard. When the dirt was patted down I suggested that we say a few words.

"For a dead mouse?" Fenton said.

"It's not Mercury's fault that he's a mouse," I pointed out.

"Wait, when did we name him Mercury?"

"Right now. No person or animal should go to his reward without having a name." I cleared my throat. "Mercury the mouse? Thank you for blessing our lives with your . . . existence. I didn't have a chance to get to know you very well, but I think that as mice go, you were one of the best. Sorry that my brother scooped out your guts, but that's how he is. I hope you enjoyed your second life, even if it was electrically weird."

Before lowering my head I stared demandingly at Fenton. He grumbled but then said, "Thanks for being part of our experiments. I hope that someday other mice will know that you were the first mouse to get two lives for the price of one."

Considering his attitude going into it, I thought that my brother did a decent job with his eulogy. At my end I tried to squeeze out a few tears to properly honor the mouse's life, but my ducts did not cooperate. Mice are disgusting, if you think about it. Especially the ones that have been gutted by curious boys playing with sharp instruments.

Chapter 29

I Kiss Luke Stambaugh
and Live to Tell about It

That Wednesday was the last day of school. There were no tests or homework assignments, lunch was pizza slices and chocolate cake, and recess was stretched out so it covered the entire afternoon.

Overall it was a pretty good day.

It started on the bus when Luke Stambaugh and his sister, Emily, boarded, and Luke sat next to me and did the usual did-our-shoes-just-accidentally-touch? thing. I watched as he twisted a lock of his blond hair, which is kind of a girl thing to do, but that didn't make it less cute.

"So I was thinking," he said, looking past me, out the window. "Would you maybe like to hang out during the summer?"

189

"The entire summer?" I said, taken by surprise. I had hoped maybe he'd ask for my email address. Hanging out together was like jumping ahead three steps.

"Or part of the summer, whatever is cool for you." He met my eyes, then quickly looked away.

"Sure," I said, "but my dad has gotten weird about people visiting our farm, so it would have to be at your house—okay?"

Luke nodded, and I did something unexpected and beyond myself—I kissed him on his cheek. I'm not saying that the world suddenly looked glittery, but I'm not saying that it didn't look glittery either.

"Whoa," he said, touching his cheek and looking stunned.

"Whoa indeed," I said, super nerdishly. Things were moving a little too fast with Luke, and I felt kind of lurchy in my stomach, like I hadn't yet adjusted to the new rate of speed.

Once we were on school grounds, Luke ignored me like he always did and met up with his friends, Matt, Jonas, and a kid called the Other Kevin, since he was one of two Kevins in our school, and the first Kevin was loads more interesting. By then I had accepted the fact that Luke was more comfortable hanging out with his tribe than with me and wanted to give his pals the impression he was girlproof.

Which meant that during recess Luke played games with his friends instead of with me. Sure, I could have wiggled my way onto his softball team, but I didn't want to make him feel weird, so I just watched him fielding grounders and running to first base, thinking, *I kissed that kid over there*. It seemed like a monumental event was being treated like an everyday thing, and I wasn't sure why.

Anyway.

I had planned to give Luke a "happy summer" gift, a tiny apple from the maple tree, before the school day ended—my way of saying here's something special for someone special—but watching Luke horse around with his friends, I decided that someone else might be more worthy of such a rare gift. I hunted for my science teacher, Mr. Embry, and found him chatting with Mr. Dinkins, the assistant principal. Getting in trouble at my school often leads to the expression, "I just got dinked by Dinkins!"

I waved my arms around to get Mr. Embry's attention. When he finally noticed, he left his colleague and shuffled up to me.

"Hello, Fiona," he said. "I actually thought I might

get through the entire last day of school without being assaulted by your latest barrage of science-related questions and inquiries, but I guess it wasn't meant to be. How are you today?"

Was that a compliment disguised as an insult, or an insult disguised as a compliment?

"I'm good," I said, butterflies of the nervous sub-species (*butterfly nervosa*) floating around inside me, for some reason. "You know, last day of school. Yippee!"

Insert awkward, rolling-my-feet-inside-my-sneakers moment.

"So guess what?" I said to Mr. Embry. "Since I won't see you for a few months, I have something I want to give you as a thanks-for-putting-up-with-me type thing." I pulled the maple apple from my jeans pocket and handed it to him.

"An apple for your teacher, how sweet," he said. "This isn't a crab apple, is it?"

"Nope, not a crab apple. Figure out what it is and win a cookie."

"What kind of cookie?"

"Oatmeal raisin. It's the one cookie I excel at baking. The key is to not overdo the raisins. I'm not sure why I'm revealing my secrets!"

Mr. Embry smiled, wished me an "incredible

summer," and returned to Mr. Dinkins while gazing at the apple with curiosity, a puzzle he had been assigned to solve.

I lingered in a state of pristine happiness for a moment, but then I realized that I might have messed up. Unlike most people, Mr. Embry had access to the equipment—Bunsen burners, microscopes, et cetera— needed to solve the mystery of the *mapple*. And what if he went public with the amazing scientific discovery and named me as the source?

I had planted a seed but was unsure if I wanted anything to grow from it.

Chapter 30

A Room without a View

Without school sucking up most of our time, Fenton and I were spending more of it with Grandpa Wade and Scruffy. Sometimes Grandpa wasn't exactly thrilled to see us, but he never did anything rude like ask us to leave so he could get back to his books.

Now that he was getting used to talking again after three years, his voice was slightly less choppy, and he'd sometimes read out loud, which usually caused Fenton to bolt due to a severe allergy to the written word. But no matter whether Grandpa was reading a chapter of a Harry Potter book or lines from *Macbeth*, I loved every second of it. For the first time in my life I had a grandparent willing to read to me. It was like finding a stash of gold when you were just about ready to stop believing in its existence.

As for Scruffy, he didn't grow any fur or flesh or replace his missing organs, and he never warmed up to my brother and me. Whatever gland in dogs was responsible for loving people just wasn't there anymore. But at least he was no longer trying to return to his grave.

Dad and Grandpa still weren't talking, but Dad did buy some new clothes for his father—including three pairs of overalls, which was what Grandpa liked to wear during his first life—and a bed on wheels and a slightly used easy chair so he'd be more comfortable in the storm cellar, and two kerosene lanterns so he could read all day without burning through flashlight batteries. To you those might sound like small things not worth mentioning, but to Fenton and me they were huge: Dad was finally acknowledging that Grandpa Wade was living with us—although in the storm cellar—and was trying to make his stay there a little bit better. That gave us hope that Dad might actually talk to Grandpa one day in a heart-to-heart way, even though Grandpa technically might not have a heart.

Overall, things had gotten pretty comfortable, except for when Grandpa Wade asked about Grandma

Jean and Uncle Jack, if we had heard from them and if they were planning to visit the farm. I'd say that I didn't have any news and quickly change the subject. Clearly, Grandpa Wade wanted to spend time with his wife and kid, but Dad, Fenton, and I hadn't figured out a way to make that happen without causing major freakage. Maybe Uncle Jack could handle seeing his undead father without flipping out, but we were worried that Grandma Jean would drop dead due to sudden fright. And then they'd be in two different places again.

I couldn't fix that problem yet, but I was able to find better housing for Grandpa. For a while, Fenton and I had been dropping hints to Dad that the storm cellar was an unsuitable place for Grandpa Wade to live and for us to visit. All those nasty spiders, we'd say, and surely the dampness was bad for our sinuses, *sniffle sniffle*. But Dad ignored us. Out of sight, out of mind was his approach to Grandpa. As long as he was tucked away in the cellar, he didn't have to deal with him directly.

One night at the dinner table, fueled by the knowledge that Grandpa Wade might not be around much longer if the light's power wore off, I decided to get pushy.

"So, Dad," I said, while we were wolfing down meatloaf and cooked carrots. "I think we should move Grandpa Wade upstairs. A storm cellar isn't a good place for a person to be living, even if that person isn't, you know, alive. It might even be against the law, having someone live in a storm cellar."

Fenton flashed a good-luck-with-that look, and Dad speared a carrot.

"You and your brother are suddenly worried about law and order?" he said. "If the cops had caught you guys the night you were at the cemetery, you would probably be in juvenile jail right now, serving out your sentences for graveyard desecration."

Okay, so he had a point, but I thought his words were kind of mean since a few weeks had passed since Fenton and I had robbed the graveyard of one of its residents.

"Actually, I'm worried about Grandpa," I said. "I think he'd be happier living in the house. It's depressing down there! Plus we have a spare bedroom. And, just so you know, last time I was in the cellar I saw a spider as big as a baseball. What if that thing bit me? I'd be one big spider bite for an entire month."

Dad finished eating his carrots, then said that Grandpa Wade living upstairs was too risky, that if someone saw him and figured out what had been happening on our little farm it could turn out bad.

"I have no idea what the light ball is," he said, "but I do know that in the wrong hands something that is generally good can be used for bad purposes. Take nuclear fission—or is it fusion?—I always mess that up. Anyway, it can be used to light cities, but it can also be used to build bombs. Not everyone is as gentle and high-minded as we are, so we need to be careful."

I hadn't thought much about the great ball of light being used for evil purposes, but I guess it was possible. What if someone used it to bring back Jack the Ripper or other famous killers?

To lessen Dad's worries, I quickly concocted a plan where we would cover the windows in the spare bedroom, and Fenton and I would make sure Grandpa Wade stayed in his room during the day. "Please?" I said, clasping my hands.

Dad looked from me to Fenton, who, miraculously, was wearing his best puppy-dog face, and back to me again, then he sort of wiggled his mouth and shrugged, his way of giving the green light without having to say the word "yes." But just as I was starting to get all happy inside, a gray cloud named Bummer appeared and stuck around awhile.

"Just because we'll be living on the same floor does not mean I have an obligation to talk to him," Dad said, stabbing a hunk of meatloaf. "You can't fix thirty years worth of bad parenting just by showing up one day, dead or alive."

From a cheerful *woo-hoo* to an unhappy *wah wah* in fifteen seconds. That had to be some kind of record.

The next day I covered the windows in the spare bedroom with bedsheets, then Fenton and I went into the storm cellar, and I gave Grandpa the good news that we were moving him upstairs.

"Fenton and Fiona Movers are here to serve you," I said, a little too gleefully. Glee always feels like a false emotion to me, like joy pumped up by a bicycle tire pump.

"Okay with . . . your dad?" Grandpa Wade said.

"It was his idea," I said. A lie, but it felt like the right thing to say.

Grandpa Wade smiled and started to gather his books, but I told him to not bother, that Fenton and I would carry them into the house. My brother made sure the coast was clear, then we took our grandfather by the arms and shuttled him out of the cellar and into the house.

Inside the spare bedroom, Grandpa Wade sat on the bed, and I went over the list of rules, most of them involving making sure he stayed hidden during the day, and to never answer the door or the phone.

"Thanks . . . warden," Grandpa said, looking around the room. "Was—Jack's room. Long time . . . ago. So many mem-ories. In this house. Not all—happy."

"I know, but now is the chance to make some new happy memories," I said. "You know, Grandpa, if you make enough happy memories, soon they will out-number the bad ones, right?"

Grandpa Wade nodded, but later when I thought about it, I wasn't sure I had said anything smart. It's not really about numbers when it comes to memo-ries, is it? Seems like one terrible memory can take up more brain space than ten happy memories. I'm not sure why the bad stuff should have so much power.

Fenton and I went and fetched Grandpa's clothes, books, and walking stick so he'd feel at home. Sadly, Scruffy had to stay in the storm cellar, but neither Grandpa Wade nor Scruffy seemed particularly upset about it. Maybe Grandpa had realized what Fenton and I had, that it wasn't easy to love a dog that had lost its soul.

Chapter 31

Oh No, There Goes My Toe

Fenton and I didn't take long to break our own rules. That afternoon we invited Grandpa Wade outside so he could "work on his tan" (ha-ha) and watch us kick a soccer ball. We brought him to the backyard through the back door so he wouldn't be seen. Daisy had wandered into the backyard and was chewing on some grass. "God's lawn mowers," Dad called the goats.

After several minutes of watching us boot the ball, Grandpa Wade asked if he could try it. When he was alive he had never kicked a soccer ball or watched a soccer match, so it would be a new experience for him.

"Did you play any sports when you were our age?" Fenton asked.

"Baseball," Grandpa Wade said. "Coulda been. A star."

"Then why didn't you try out for the pros?" my brother asked. "Or did you?"

Grandpa Wade shook his head. "Those days . . . future set. Came from farmers. Would be farmer. No baseball. No college. No need."

Sometimes I don't appreciate all the options I have for my future until I hear someone, usually an old person, say how few opportunities they had when they were young. If you were a boy and your dad was a farmer you became a farmer, and so on. In my life, not once has my dad suggested a future career for me. With my mom, I know she would love it if I became a writer, which could happen, but if I ever write an article about fashion or makeup for a ladies' magazine, please find me and smack some sense into me—not too hard! Thanks in advance.

Grandpa stood and I passed the ball to him. He twisted his right foot farther than feet were supposed to bend and kicked the ball. It only went a few feet, but he seemed pleased with himself. I booted the ball to Fenton, and he kicked it to Grandpa, and for a little while we had a three-way kick going.

"So Grandpa," I said, "do you have any regrets about not chasing your dream to become a major-league baseball player?"

"Have . . . million regrets," he said. "Not about—being farmer. Or starting family. My two. Smart moves."

That was kind of cool, I thought, that a man who could have maybe been a famous baseball player was happy that he became a farmer and a family man instead.

I kicked the ball to Grandpa. He booted it, said, "Oops," and sat down on a lawn chair. He removed his right shoe and sock, then he shook his second to smallest toe out of the sock. It just sort of sat there on the grass.

"Oh well," he said. "Didn't need . . . toe anyway."

"Maybe we could, uh, tape it back on," Fenton said. I had an immediate image of Grandpa Wade held together by an entire roll of duct tape. It was hard to keep a straight face.

Grandpa put his sock and shoe on, and I was stuck in one of those don't want to/can't stop myself situations where I very much did *not* want to look at Grandpa Wade's discarded toe, yet it was all I could seem to do.

But then I noticed out of the corner of my eye a strange movement near the grove of apple and peach trees—wait a minute! It was Sonny Baskins, climbing the fence that separated our properties from our side, like he had been in our yard and was returning to his own property!

What was Sonny doing in our yard? I wondered. And did he see Grandpa Wade? Answers to those questions came later, and they weren't good ones.

I can't tell you a lot about Sonny Baskins, since I don't know much. But Dad did tell Fenton and me a while back that when he and Uncle Jack were growing up on the farm, Sonny used to be a pretty good neighbor—was even friendly at times. Dad and Jack and our grandparents would sometimes have a two-family barbecue with Sonny and his people, and even though Sonny's three boys were older than my dad and uncle, now and then they all played sports together, or engaged in hijinks like tossing rotten apples at cars passing by on the road.

But then things started to fall apart for Sonny, Dad told us. His wife divorced him and moved herself and the boys halfway across the state, so Sonny hardly ever saw his kids. And then the oldest boy was killed in the war in Iraq, the first one. So Sonny Baskins became a cranky old coot who kept to himself, and even though he wasn't a danger to Fenton and me, we thought, he *was* a serious threat to our sporting goods supply. Dad had warned us that if a ball we were tossing or kicking ended up in Sonny's yard, we should just leave it there. Last count, Sonny owed us two Wiffle balls, a kickball, a mini football, and a Frisbee.

Anyway.

I pointed Sonny Baskins out to Fenton, then told Grandpa that we better go inside. We helped him up, and he hobbled to the house with the help of his walking stick.

Once Grandpa Wade was safely in his room, I found a plastic zipper bag and returned outside to retrieve the toe, a perfectly normal thing for a twelve-year-old girl to do. But I couldn't find it anywhere. I checked the part of the lawn where we had played soccer. Again, nothing.

I looked over at Sonny's property. Had he snagged the toe and run off? That could be bad.

Then I saw Daisy, chewing on grass. Hmm. Maybe *she* ate the toe? Ick! Double ick! But it'd be better if that were the case than Sonny Baskins finding it. But still . . . ick!

Chapter 32

Grandpa's Secret

I decided that during dinner I would tell Dad about Sonny Baskins spying on us. I had put off saying anything about Sonny's earlier snooping because I was worried that Dad would flip out and say we needed to rebury Grandpa Wade and Scruffy and chop down the miracle tree to protect ourselves from outsiders with bad intentions.

My plan caved in when Dad phoned to say that he was heading to the Ice Queen's house for dinner and he'd be home about nine. I almost blurted that it was *urgent* he come home immediately so we could talk, but I didn't want to freak him out ahead of a bigger freak-out when he found out about Sonny Baskins. So I just said that I hoped he didn't come home too late so we'd have time to catch up on the day's events. Lame, I know.

After hanging up I felt tied up inside, so I went to the dusty attic and dug the barrel jar out of the box of Christmas junk, and held the light to my stomach. Slowly the ropes came undone. Maybe it was all in my head, but I always seemed to be at a calmer frequency when close to the light ball, my worries shrinking down until they were almost too small to see.

I had been holding the light ball for about a minute when that weird thing happened where it seemed like it was talking directly to my brain.

Ask Grandpa, the light said.

"Ask Grandpa what?" I said. But the light kept saying *Ask Grandpa* like it was stuck in a loop.

Confused, but curious, I put the jar away, went downstairs, knocked on Grandpa Wade's door, and let myself in. He was reading Shakespeare aloud, which he'd started doing as way of working on his voice, trying to smooth out the hiccups. Here's the cleaned-up version of what he was reading, from Shakespeare's eighteenth sonnet.

> . . . Sometime too hot the eye of heaven shines,
>   And often is his gold complexion dimmed;

And every fair from fair sometime declines,
By chance, or nature's changing course
untrimmed;
But thy eternal summer shall not fade,
Nor lose possession of that fair thou ow'st,
Nor shall death brag thou wander'st in his shade,
When in eternal lines to time thou grow'st,
So long as men can breathe, or eyes can see,
So long lives this, and this gives life to thee.

"That's lovely," I said, feeling glittery in my cells and wishing that Luke Stambaugh spoke to me in that Shakespearean way.

"If you . . . told me, past life," he said. "One day quoting Shake-speare. Called you . . . loon."

I smiled. "Um, Grandpa. Do you know something about the ball of light that you haven't told me?"

"No," he quickly said, burying his head in the book, a clear case of Avoiding Reality Syndrome.

"Are you sure? Because when I was holding the light jar, I sort of got the idea you might know something."

"Like me to read . . . Sonnet Nineteen?"

"Sure. Right after you answer my question."

Grandpa Wade thought for a moment (or at least he was doing that sideways-eyes thing), then he patted the bed. I sat down and he told me a story. For your sake I cut out the annoying dots and dashes.

After you and Freddy [he meant Fenton] *dug me up at the cemetery, it took me a few minutes to get my bearings. I guess you could say it was like being born: I was trying to figure out where I was and who I was and what I was doing there.*

Once I saw the light ball on my chest I thought, Well, that makes sense. *You see, Fiona, this was not my first encounter with the light ball. The story I am about to tell you I have never told anyone, so I'd like you to keep it a secret, okay?*

[Here was where I nodded and crossed my fingers, which canceled my nod and what it might have implied.]

This happened a long time ago when your father was four, and Jack would have been two. Even though Jean hated it when I did this because of the risk, sometimes I took the boys for tractor rides while I was tilling or mowing, or just for the fun of going for a ride across the acreage. That day, Jean had taken Jack into Red Lodge for a doctor's appointment, so I was alone with Will. And yes, I might have been slightly drunk, even though it was early afternoon. I was never a strong person when it came to alcohol.

Anyway, we were near the beet field, Will on my lap, when it started to rain, so I decided to head back. But as I turned the tractor it jerked, and I lost hold of Will. He fell off my lap and landed on the ground. Before I could apply the brakes and kill the engine there was a terrible thud as one of the rear wheels rolled over him. Fortunately, I didn't have the tiller or mower attached that day, or it's possible that none of us would be here.

[Here was where I got queasy, imagining a big tractor wheel rolling over my father when he was a kid.]

I hopped off the tractor and went to Will: he was limp, didn't move a muscle. I was pretty sure he was dead. I thought of lifting him up and trying to shake life back into him, but what if he was barely alive but had a broken back? Picking him up could have paralyzed him for life.

So instead, as the storm rolled in, I opened my arms to the heavens and said, "Please, God, save my boy, and I will give up drinking and be the most loving and generous husband, father, neighbor, and citizen ever."

I was sure my words would do no good—this was real life, not the movies—so I was about to run to the house and call for an ambulance, when a huge blast of lightning struck the ground not ten feet from where I stood, electrifying my hair and scaring me silly.

I thought that God was trying to wipe me out for accidentally killing my kid, but then the strangest thing happened: a ball made of light shot out of the ground and landed on Will, and for about ten seconds his body glowed. I

thought I was seeing things, like sometimes happens with drunks.

The ball disappeared into the ground before reappearing a minute later, near where Will lay. That was when your father began to stir, and I realized that he was alive. "Thank you, God!" I shouted, tears pouring out of me. I went to your father and helped him sit up. He looked around dazed-like and asked what had happened, so I told him that he had fallen off the tractor. I did a quick inspection, and the only damage I could find was a bruise near his spine. I was certain that a miracle had just happened. At the very least he should have had several broken bones.

It was raining heavy now, and lightning was flashing, so I scooped up Will and ran to the house, where I dried him off and helped him change his clothes. I also said something to Will about not telling his mother about the tractor accident, since she'd raise a holy stink for an entire month, and he agreed. The boys loved their mother, but those days they loved me even more. I was the guy who took them for tractor rides and pony rides. For a while I could do no wrong by my sons. Then, after I broke my promise to God and became a drunk again, I could do no right.

After the rain stopped, I went to fetch the tractor and saw that the light ball was where I had left it. "Thanks for saving my boy," I said to it. "You can return to the sky now."

But the ball didn't go anywhere. So I shrugged, hopped onto the tractor, and drove to the barn. The light bounced along, following me like a dog might. It was the craziest thing.

It looked like I wasn't going to shake the light ball, and I didn't want Jean to find it and ask questions, so I put it inside a clay jar and buried it in a place I could easily remember should tragedy strike and I need the ball again, ten paces east of the maple tree in the front yard.

As the years passed, Jean and the boys stayed healthy, and when an animal we liked died, I decided to let nature take its course instead of trying to bring it back with the light ball. It felt like I was in possession of something that no man should own, and I was wary of ever using it again. Eventually I forgot about it being buried in the front yard, or at least I didn't think about it very often. And then, the night at the cemetery when you and Freddy [he meant Fenton] *dug me up and I saw it beating on my chest, it all came back to me.*

There's something important I want to say to you, Fiona, so please pay close attention. I don't know if my pleading to the heavens for your father's life to be saved had anything to do with the light ball falling from the sky and doing what it did, or if it was a random event. Every hour of every day, somewhere on Earth a desperate parent is pleading to God to save their sick or injured child, and sometimes it's not going to end in a good way. So why was Will spared instead of some other kid? We Norths are no better or worse than anyone else. Miracles do occur, I saw one of them up close, but they are as rare as white buffalos. I can't explain that either, why miracles are not more common and seem to be dished out randomly.

And there's this: having a say in who or what lives or is brought back—that's not something meant for people, and could ruin a person if it went to his head. I sure as heck didn't want that power, which was another reason I left the light ball buried in the front yard. So I hope that you and your father and brother will think twice before using it again. We are just a bunch of nobodies. Let someone else be blessed by it for a change.

Finished with the story, Grandpa Wade hid his face in his hands. Sometimes sharing secrets brings relief, and other times it causes misery. My grandfather was looking pretty miserable.

And I was gobsmacked. If Grandpa's words were true, Dad, Fenton, and I owed our lives to the great ball of light: if it hadn't saved Dad, my brother and I would have never been born. I was the child of a miracle, and so was Fenton, and that seemed almost too much to deal with. Why couldn't I just be a normal kid instead of someone special? A lot is expected of miracle kids, that they return the favor to the world and be happy people who have a positive influence on those around them. But what if I want to be a grumpy writer who lives in a shack somewhere and keeps to herself?

I also realized that I needed to rethink everything I knew about the light ball. For starters, it didn't ride a lightning bolt down from the sky the day of the storm, but was freed from the ground when lightning struck the exact right spot. (And was that random, or did the lightning somehow know to strike our yard?)

It gave me chills, thinking about the great ball of light being buried in the front yard for thirty-two years, waiting for another chance to perform a miracle.

But what really weirded me out was when I thought about circles and cycles, how the light first appeared when Grandpa Wade pleaded that my father's life be saved, and then, thirty-two years later, Fenton and I used the same light ball to bring back our grandfather, the man who had summoned the light.

And why us?—like Grandpa had said. Why should we have a guardian angel in the shape of a ball? That made no sense. We weren't special, and surely there were thousands of families in greater need of an angel than us. WHY US?

"Dad never told me about the tractor accident," I said to my grandpa.

Grandpa Wade unfolded himself and looked at me. "He was . . . four. Don't think . . . he remembers. Probably good, not remember-ing . . . dying."

"You could be right," I said, "but I think you should tell him the story, and don't leave anything out. Maybe it will help you guys fix things."

"Or . . . worsen them," he said, explaining he was worried that what Dad would take away from the story was that his drunken father let go of him during a tractor ride and he had been killed when he was run over by a wheel. "Your dad . . . look at me. And see. His drunken killer. I couldn't. Handle . . . that."

He picked up the Shakespeare book and started reading it out loud. Not being a total dope, I took it as a signal that he wanted me to leave.

"Enjoy Sonnet Nineteen," I said with annoyance as I left his room. So Shakespeare could write a little, big deal. It wasn't like he was family.

I Impersonate a Balloon

After leaving Grandpa Wade I roamed the house, down the hall and from room to room, like I was floating a few inches above the carpet. Gravity? Where are you, buddy?

"I'm here because of the light," I kept saying to myself. And each time I said that sentence it added more helium. I was in danger of floating up to the ceiling and staying there until I deflated.

Hoping for answers, I went to the attic, pulled the barrel jar from the Christmas box, and held it to my chest.

"So you really saved my dad's life when he was four?" I asked.

Pulse-pulse.

"And Dad and Fenton and I wouldn't be alive today if you hadn't done that?"

Pulse-pulse.

"And Grandpa buried you in the front yard, and you stayed there for thirty-two years until the lightning strike set you free?"

Pulse-pulse.

Despite my efforts, which included *intense mental focus*, I could not connect to the light ball and do the mind-to-mind thought-transfer thing, like we were on different wavelengths.

Frustrated, I set the jar in the box and went and bugged Fenton. He was in his room, reading a Thor comic book.

"What now?" he said. "I'm kind of busy."

"Grandpa just told me a really weird story," I said. "It might interest—"

"You had me at 'weird,'" he interrupted, closing the comic book and giving me his full attention.

So I told him the story. He closely listened, but didn't react much. Coming to the end, I wondered if Fenton would have been more deeply affected if he had heard it from Grandpa Wade instead of from me.

"Now you know the truth," I said. "The light ball didn't fall from the sky, but was in our yard the whole time, waiting for us to find it and use it. Is that whacked, or what?"

Fenton scratched an ear. "So you're saying that if Dad hadn't fallen off the tractor and gotten run over, and everything that happened after that, you and I wouldn't be here today? Do I have that right?"

"That's part of it," I said. "The much bigger part is Grandpa shouting to the heavens, and the ball of light showing up and doing its thing. And then Grandpa buried it, and it stayed buried for thirty-two years, until we, the kids who would have never been born without the light's help, captured the light on the day of the storm, then used it so we could bring back Grandpa Wade, the man responsible for the light being in our yard in the first place. Isn't that amazing?"

Circles and cycles, I thought. *Circles and cycles.*

"Sure, but you need to go back one step, to Dad falling off the tractor and getting run over," Fenton said. "If he had stayed on Grandpa's lap the whole time and is never run over, maybe his life changes in a different way, and he never meets Mom, and we never get born, and we never dig up Grandpa and Scruffy. You know, the caterpillar effect. Change one thing and the whole world changes in response."

"It's called the butterfly effect," I said.

The more I thought about it, I realized Fenton was right. If our father had stayed on the tractor that day, never gotten run over and then resuscitated, it would not have guaranteed that Fenton and I would one day be born, even though our dad had stayed alive the entire time. It *might* have guaranteed that none of us would have an encounter with the great ball of light, but even that I was not sure of. Change one thing and the entire world reshuffles itself. Crazy how that works, eh?

While I was thinking through all of that, Fenton picked up the comic book and waved me away. I wanted to pinch him. Why couldn't we have kept exploring Deep and Meaningful Caverns a little while longer?

The Truth Will Give You the Giggles

When my dad said he'd be home by nine, he really meant he'd be home by ten, or eleven, or twelve. I didn't usually get too upset about his lateness because I knew he intended to keep his word, but then the Ice Queen did her little voodoo thing, and nine o'clock became midnight.

That night, Dad came home at twelve thirty, but it wasn't a problem because I was still awake, trying to figure out stuff like life and death, and circles and cycles and fate, and how the ball of light fit into all of it. As usual, I came up with some really good questions. What was missing was answers.

"Hey there, pumpkin pie, what are you doing up so late?" Dad said, stepping inside the house and looking sleepy eyed.

I gave him a quick hug. "I've been waiting for you. There's something you and Grandpa need to settle this minute." I took his hand and led him to his father's room. I had to do some serious arm pulling the closer we got.

"This isn't the right time for this," Dad tried, but I was having none of it.

"Go in there," I instructed my father, "and ask Grandpa Wade to tell you the story he told me earlier tonight—every word. And don't come out until you've talked it through. Seriously, I'm not letting you out until you have finished talking."

"Honey, I know you mean well," he said, a smidge more firmly, "but this is a bad idea. First, it's late and I'm tired. Second, I probably don't want to hear whatever it is your grandfather has to say."

Any other time I probably would have grumbled and walked away, defeated. But that night I felt more sure of myself than usual. And I knew what needed to happen.

"Dad," I said, "you know that I think you are awesome, but when it comes to dealing with your father you are being a big baby. If you don't want to talk to him for your sake and his sake, then do it for Fenton and me. The iciness between you two is messing us up."

How could he say no to that?

I knocked on the door, pushed it open a little, and let

go of Dad's hand. "You really need to trust me," I said.

Dad gave me a steady gaze that I interpreted as meaning *Maybe I should have raised llamas instead of kids*, let out an unhappy sigh, and stepped across the threshold. I quickly pulled the door closed then leaned against it, wanting to hear every word, and hoping I just sent Dad to a peace conference, not a battlefield. It was like locking up two jungle cats and hoping they became friends.

It took a minute before Grandpa started talking, and, curse the thick door and walls, I could only hear a few words like "tractor" and "storm" and "screwed up." I did hear Dad say "oh dear lord," but there are different kinds of *oh dear lord*s, including the kind you cry out when a coyote just ate your poodle, and the kind you shout when you win the lottery—I wasn't sure which this one was. Though I guessed, considering the topic, that a coyote had just eaten a poodle.

While I strained to listen, Fenton stumbled out of his room in his pajamas, running a hand through his hair and yawning so wide I could see his tonsils.

"What's going on?" he asked, bumbling along.

"Dad and Grandpa are talking about the day of the tractor accident," I reported.

He stopped walking and looked at me. "Huh. I guess if they kill each other, Uncle Jack can raise us."

He continued to the kitchen, found a box of graham crackers, and returned to his room.

"Save some for me," I said, wondering why I bothered to say those words. Whenever a box or bag of a snack food was taken inside Fenton's room, its fate was sealed. That kid was making a serious dent in the national food supply.

After fifteen minutes of catching the odd loud word here and there, it suddenly grew quiet in Grandpa Wade's room—all I heard were some sniffles from Dad and a wheezy sound from Grandpa Wade. And then Dad said something to Grandpa and began sobbing. His crying tripped tears in me.

When my father suddenly opened the door, I wiped at my eyes with my shirt and pretended I was inspecting the hall for evidence of termites. Dad stood in the doorway for a moment. He looked kind of . . . shipwrecked: wild hair, wet eyes, and a bit unsteady.

"How'd it go in there?" I asked, returning my eyes to the baseboard.

And that was when Dad smothered me with a warm, melting-butter kind of hug.

"You know something, Fiona?" he said, near the end of the hug. "I've been such an idiot, holding on to things that I should have let go of a long time ago. Thank you for helping me see that. Your grandfather . . . He has his faults, too many of them to list if we don't want to be up all night. But, well, family is family, so we ought to try to love each other no matter what, right?"

I didn't know what to say—this had turned out much better than I had expected. My face was pressed against Dad's chest, anyway, so it was not exactly ideal conditions for speaking.

Dad kissed me on the top of the head, exhaled hard, and went inside his room—it looked like he had a lot he wanted to think about. I stood there shaking for a moment, feeling overwhelmed by . . . everything.

When I recovered enough to walk, I went into the kitchen and drank some grape juice and wolfed down a powdered donut. And then I headed to my room, passing by Grandpa's room on my right and Dad's room on my left. Feeling suddenly super happy about what had happened, that they had *actually talked things out*, I started giggling, and then I seemed to have trouble finding the off switch. Has that ever happened to you? So I hurried into my room, slammed the door shut, dove onto the bed, covered my head with a pillow, and laughed until I was all out of giggles.

It's rare, but sometimes laughter can be a tiny bit scary. Feel free to disagree!

Chapter 35

A Zombie Makeover

The next morning at the breakfast table Dad
announced that he had made a decision, that on
Sunday we would free the light ball in the Beartooth
Mountains, which were part of Gallatin National
Forest, a few miles west of us. He hoped that the light
would return to the sky and leave us alone, or find
some other family to "bug" with its miracles.

Fenton protested—what if there was an accident
a year from now and we were suddenly in need of
another miracle?—and Grandpa Wade looked doubt-
ful, but I had switched to Dad's side. The great ball of
light probably belonged up in the sky, not on Earth.
And even if it did belong in the world, our family had
hogged it for too long.

Dad then repeated an earlier thought that owning the light ball could cause harm to our family if word got out and people tried to get their hands on it. I remembered that I hadn't told him about Sonny Baskins spying on us, but my new thought was that in two days the light ball would be gone, and with it any dangers.

Before we ditched the light ball, Dad thought we should tell Grandma Jean, Uncle Jack, and the Ice Queen everything, starting with the tractor accident when Dad was four and continuing to the night Fenton and I dug up Grandpa Wade. Instead of all at once, we'd tell Grandma Jean later that day, and then Jack and the Ice Queen would get the news at different times on Saturday.

"Your grandmother and uncle are family," Dad said, "and in two months Beverly will also be part of our family. So it would be wrong to keep such big secrets from them. But we need to be smart. There is only one ambulance serving rural Carbon County. If we have three people faint or suffer cardiac trouble at the same time due to sudden shock, it could be catastrophic. Better to space it out, I think."

Grandpa Wade looked worried. "Seeing me . . . bad idea. I'm ugly. Might . . . scare 'em away."

"Don't worry, Grandpa," I said. "We'll fix you up so you look like a movie star."

"Which movie?" he said, smiling crookedly. "*Frank-en-stein* or . . . *Night of the . . . Living Dead*?"

That was pretty funny, I thought, but it was also kind of sad, because my grandfather thought of himself as a monster, which he only was on the outside. Later, I wrote this in my science notebook: *even dead people can have self-esteem issues.*

After breakfast, Dad and I drove to Red Lodge to pick up supplies so we could improve Grandpa Wade's appearance. At Mountain Pharmacy we bought makeup, press-on fingernails, and sunglasses. At a thrift shop run by a Lutheran church we found a brown wig, an old-style man's hat, and a Freddy Kruger mask (we were only interested in the rubber nose).

"There should be a guide available on how to make zombies look more like living people," Dad complained as we searched through bins at the thrift shop.

"True, but we are the first people to ever do this." I pulled a polka-dotted tie out of a bin and showed it to Dad, but he shook his head. Perfect for a clown, he said, but not right for his dad. Happiness surged through me—he truly cared about his father, and was hoping things went well when it came time to introduce him to Grandma Jean, Uncle Jack, and Beverly.

"You seem sort of happy since you guys had your talk," I mentioned, trying to be casual.

He nodded. "Overall, I'm glad he's here and living with us. But it's kind of sad, if you think about it."

"What do you mean?"

"That it took death to inspire your grandfather to become a better person. If that inspiration had happened while he was alive, he'd probably still be alive. I mean *alive*-alive. Why'd he have to die first before he changed his ways?"

That was one of those questions I wasn't expected to answer, which was good, since I didn't have a clue.

Once home, it was time for an extreme makeover. Grandpa Wade sat on a chair in the kitchen, while Dad, Fenton, and I went to work. It was kind of like we were getting Grandpa ready for a Halloween party, only the goal was to make him look less scary instead of more scary.

Dad put the wig on Grandpa Wade's head and we all cracked up. You don't often see zombies with long flowing brown hair. Dad decided he'd be in charge of trimming the wig.

Fenton was on nose duty, which involved cutting the nose out of the Freddy mask and pasting it onto what was left of Grandpa's nose. It looked weird and rubbery, but at least no bones were showing.

My job was to stick fake nails on Grandpa's fingers, and to paint his face and neck with makeup, like I had vast knowledge of press-on nails and makeup due to the fact that I was a girl. Kind of sexist if you ask me, but I didn't complain since I was having fun, and Grandpa Wade seemed to be enjoying the attention.

"Feel like . . . celebrity," he said as we fussed over him. "Old. Dead. Ugly. Celeb-rity."

"You are beautiful in your own special way," I said, which was not really true, but it was a nice thing to say.

When the makeover was finished, Dad took a few pictures of Fenton and me posing with Grandpa Wade, then I took one of him and Grandpa. "Say cheese," I said before snapping the picture, but instead they said "Gouda," a kind of cheese, which, I learned, was what they used to say when Grandma Jean snapped photos of them and Jack. Now I know why all the old pictures of my dad, Grandpa, and Uncle Jack look like they're whistling!

After looking at the pictures I decided to not show them to Grandpa Wade. Despite the makeover he was still ugly, but at least it was a might-be-able-to-pass-for-a-living-person kind of ugly. So maybe Grandma Jean wouldn't drop dead when she saw her undead husband up close. But if she did croak, at least we had a way to revive her.

Chapter 36

Surprise!

At five o'clock Dad went to fetch Grandma Jean. He had invited her over for dinner, saying there were important matters he wished to discuss with her. His plan was to tell her about the tractor accident and the ball of light while on their way to our farm, and then spring Grandpa Wade on her when she arrived. What could go wrong?

"Be extra loving and well behaved," Dad said to Fenton and me before tramping to his SUV. "We are about to give your grandmother the biggest shock of her life. We will need to be there for her, no matter how it goes."

In other words, several sticks of dynamite had been placed in our house. But the good news was that no one had lit the fuses yet.

Fenton and I stayed behind because Grandpa Wade, who hadn't seen his wife in three years, was a nervous wreck. It was our duty to try to keep him calm and hopeful.

"Should move . . . back. To cellar," Grandpa said, adjusting his hat as I held a mirror in front of him. "Or grave. Better . . . hiding places."

"Nah, stay here with us," I said, smiling encouragingly. "We got sunshine. And TV!"

"But what if . . . Jean. Doesn't like me. No more?" he asked.

"No reason to worry, Grandpa," I said. "You were married to her for nearly forty years. She wouldn't have stayed with you that long if she didn't love you."

"Wasn't always . . . nice to Jean," he said, looking away.

"And now is your chance to make up for that and be super nice to her," I said, setting down the mirror and picking up face powder—his rubber nose needed more work.

Grandpa Wade wanted some time alone to "get his head together," so Fenton and I went outside and sat on the porch. Dad and Grandma Jean were due any minute.

"I'm super nervous for Grandpa," I said. "What if Grandma is, well, grossed out and rejects him? He's a corpse!"

"Or she could reject him for a different reason," he said.

"What do you mean?"

"Well, I was just thinking, what if Grandma loved Grandpa *because* he was a drunk."

"That makes no sense. Why would anyone love a drunk more than a sober person?"

He shrugged. "Well, what if Grandma Jean enjoyed the fact that she had someone to take care of—her drunken husband. She'd feed him and yell at him and try to keep him from doing stupid stuff, just like she would if he was her kid. So she was needed, since Grandpa Wade couldn't take care of himself when drunk. And maybe that's the reason they stayed together so long. If Grandpa had been sober, Grandma Jean wouldn't have been needed as much."

I was thinking about what Fenton said, sort of jealous that he had an insightful thought that should have come from my brain, when suddenly—

"Kids! Help!" Grandpa Wade cried from inside the house.

We rushed inside and found Grandpa in the

kitchen, leaking fluid from his chest and armpits, and from a tiny hole in his neck. I then saw a beer can in the sink. My heart sank and my brain started sizzling.

"Grandpa!" I said. "How could you?" In a weak moment, Grandpa Wade had guzzled beer with the hope of calming his fears about how the meeting with his wife would go, and now it was dripping out of him and messing up his shirt.

"I know . . . screwed up," he said. "Please help . . . change shirt."

"Okay, but first you need to swear off booze for the rest of your second life," I said.

Grandpa Wade lowered his head and raised his right hand. "I swear. Am done . . . with booze. Forever."

I nodded, but wondered how many times he had made that exact same vow during his first life. What was it about alcohol that made it tough for some people to keep away from it? Even zombies!

Fenton ran for a towel and a new shirt for Grandpa Wade, and I poured the rest of the beer down the drain and placed the can in the recycling bin. When my brother returned, we cleaned up Grandpa Wade and helped him put on his shirt, seconds before we heard Dad's car rolling up the driveway. I told Grandpa

Wade to go hide in his room, then Fenton and I hurried out of the house.

"Welcome to the end of the world," my brother said with doomsday certainty as we skipped down the porch steps.

"Or the start of a new one," I said, with pioneer spirit.

At the car Fenton and I got some quality shoulder patting from Grandma Jean. She didn't seem particularly upset, and I wondered how much Dad had told her about the light ball, Grandpa Wade, the tractor accident, and everything else.

"I'm still not sure why I was dragged out of my apartment," Grandma said, looking around, "but it's always nice to see the farm again. Spent the best years of my life here, and also some of the worst."

Dad pointed to the miracle tree, and we headed that way. I pulled my father aside and asked what he had said to his mother.

"Only about the tree coming back to life after it was struck by lightning," he whispered. "I panicked. Sorry!"

Grandma Jean touched a maple leaf and glanced at Fenton and me. "For some reason your grandfather had an affinity for this tree. I'd see him gazing at it from the house or the porch, and often he'd set a chair near the tree and read his farm magazines there. I never understood what he saw in the tree. In my mind, a tree is a tree is a tree."

Maybe, I thought, what drew Grandpa Wade to the tree was not the tree itself, but the light ball buried close to it—the light ball that had saved his kid.

Grandma said she wanted to get out of the sun and marched to the house. Dad, Fenton, and I instantly switched to freak-out mode: Grandma Jean was supposed to be better prepared for what was waiting inside, but Dad had messed up—not that I could blame him. How do you even start that conversation? *So guess what . . .*

"Mom?" Dad said as Grandma Jean climbed the porch steps ahead of us. "Before we go inside, there are a few things I'd like to tell you."

"Nonsense, you can tell me inside," she said. "Too much sun! Too many bugs!"

She flung open the screen door. Dad, Fenton, and I tried to scoot in front of her, hoping to shield her in case Grandpa Wade hadn't stayed in his room. But we were too late. Grandpa was standing in the hall, looking, um, deadish.

Grandma Jean's jaw fell open. She gasped and

pointed to her husband. "That's . . . that's Wade. That's my Wade!"

"What's left . . . of me," Grandpa said, apparently trying to lighten the mood, which, at that moment, weighed eight hundred thousand metric tons.

My grandma suddenly got a little wobbly, so Dad helped her to the couch. Sitting, she rubbed at her temples. Dad told me to fetch a glass of water—I quickly did that. Grandma Jean downed it in three big gulps.

Meanwhile Grandpa Wade stood uneasily in the hallway, looking even more uncomfortable than his wife did. "I . . . better go," he said, turning toward his room. I felt overwhelmed with sadness for him.

But then Grandma Jean peered at her husband and firmly said, "No, come sit with me." Grandpa Wade, not willing to risk a smile, hobbled toward his wife; he didn't have his walking stick so it took a minute. He then sat on the couch, close to her.

Insert the most awkward moment ever.

"So what took you so long?" Grandma Jean said to Grandpa Wade in a scolding kind of way. "I've been waiting for you since the day you died!"

decorative chapter banner

Chapter 37

True Love Always

So get this: Grandma Jean had been expecting Grandpa Wade to return to her since shortly after his burial, though she was expecting his ghost, not a zombie. Isn't that kind of cool?

"You *are* dead, aren't you?" she asked her husband.

"Am dead," Grandpa Wade said, sounding embarrassed. "Or so I've . . . been told."

Now here is where you might want to say "aww." Grandma Jean told us that when she married Grandpa Wade they changed their vows to read "and not even death will keep us apart," instead of the usual "until death do us part." They must have been crazy in love back then, trying to extend their romance to the afterlife.

I'm not the most romantic girl in the world, usually switch the channel or flip some pages when the boy and girl characters are about to trade spit molecules. But hearing my grandmother talk about the "eternal bond" she had forged with Grandpa Wade, I was getting a bit soft and doughy—chocolate chip cookie dough? That was me.

"A promise is a promise," Grandma said to Grandpa, wiping a tear from her eye. "I guess you could say I've been living in stasis, waiting for you to return and keep your promise. I kept wondering what was taking you so long. I even said aloud sometimes, 'Where are you, Wade? You vowed to never leave me, and I have the signed contract.'"

Grandpa Wade looked overwhelmed—a steady tremble rattled his bones. When he took his wife's hand it caused tears to launch in all of us, except for Grandpa, of course, who was unable to make tears.

"I remembered my promise," he said, shaking. "But needed . . . help. To keep it."

"Well. Of course! But—oh my heavens," Grandma glanced from Dad to Fenton and me. "Is this even real? Am I dreaming?"

"It's not a dream, Grandma," I said. "As far as Grandpa Wade leaving his grave, part of it is my doing and Fenton's doing, and another part . . . Well, I guess I'll have to show you." I looked to Dad. He gave an *okay* nod so I raced up to the attic, fetched the barrel jar, raced back to the living room, and handed it to Grandma.

"What is this?" she said, slowly turning the jar, examining the light ball from different angles. "It looks like a star that fell to Earth."

"Pretty close," I said. I then nodded at Dad, encouraging him to tell the story—it seemed more like his story than it did mine or Fenton's.

He blew his nose and told his mother the entire story, only taking tiny breaks to breathe and to sniffle.

"And that's everything I know about the light ball and what it has done," he said. "Dad and I wouldn't be here if not for this thing—and you'd have no grandchildren. I'm grateful, but we need to set it free, and that's the plan for this Sunday. It's time to share it with the rest of the world."

Fenton was still against the idea—he wanted to do more experiments—but the rest of us agreed. In my head I saw the ball of light hopping around the globe, performing miracle after miracle, saving kids and adults and puppies and camels. But there was also a chance that once it was freed, it would never be seen on Earth again.

Grandma Jean, tears rolling down her cheeks, held up the ball and said, "Thank you for saving Will and for bringing back Wade. Thank you so much."

The light ball quickened its pulsation for a moment, as if it were saying something to Grandma Jean. *You're welcome*, maybe?

Grandma handed the jar to me, retook Grandpa's hand, and smiled at him in a so-good-to-see-you-again kind of way. And then the most romantic thing ever in the history of the universe happened. Grandpa Wade went to one knee and spoke to his wife the sonnet from Shakespeare he had become obsessed with.

But after saying the last lines of Sonnet 18—"So long as men can breathe, or eyes can see, / so long lives this, and this gives life to thee"—he surprised all of us by launching a second sonnet, this one by a poet named Elizabeth Barrett Browning. Here's the smooth version:

> How do I love thee? Let me count the ways.
> I love thee to the depth and breadth and height
> My soul can reach, when feeling out of sight
> For the ends of Being and ideal Grace.

I love thee to the level of every day's
Most quiet need, by sun and candle-light.
I love thee freely, as men strive for Right;
I love thee purely, as they turn from Praise.
I love thee with a passion put to use
In my old griefs, and with my childhood's faith.
I love thee with a love I seemed to lose
With my lost saints,—I love thee with the breath,
Smiles, tears, of all my life!—and, if God choose,
I shall but love thee better after death.

Grandpa Wade kissed his wife's hand, took a minute to crank himself back up out of his crouch, then sat beside her, scooting closer so their knees touched. A total Luke Stambaugh move!

The rest of us lost it, even Fenton, who normally keeps his emotions bottled up. The thing that was slapping us silly, I think, was that we had learned that

243

it wasn't just a poet's words, that love *could* survive death. And we had the living and undead proof, right there in our living room, sitting on the couch.

Wade and Jean, true love always. They said it *and* meant it.

My grandmother stayed for another hour before asking Dad to drive her home. She said that seeing her undead husband had exhausted her, and she needed time to "process the reality of the situation."

Before leaving the house, Grandma Jean hugged Grandpa Wade but she didn't kiss him—can you blame her for not wanting to kiss a dead guy? Before getting into Dad's car, Grandma warmly hugged and kissed Fenton and me, possibly for the first time. And I was struck by a thought: *and now I have a real grandmother, too.*

"We should start doing weekly visits," Grandma said to Dad as she climbed inside the SUV. "Or even twice weekly. When it comes down to it, family is the one thing that always matters."

Slipping behind the wheel, Dad shot Fenton and me a happily baffled look, like he wasn't sure he recognized the woman seated next to him as his mother. I felt the same way. It was as if Grandpa Wade had busted through Grandma Jean's defenses and made her human again. I hoped that it would stick.

As they drove off, I glanced over at Sonny Baskins's property. Sure enough, Sonny was standing in his yard, watching us. He didn't avert his eyes, even after I gave him a snarly look. I thought with all my thinking power, *Go away, Sonny Baskins, and leave us alone.* But Sonny didn't leave us alone, and that was about to become a huge problem.

Anyway.

Grandpa Wade greeted Fenton and me as we entered the house, slicking back his fake hair.

"Still got it," he said. "Still . . . ladies man."

I laughed, then I went and gave my grandfather a careful hug. "Congratulations, Grandpa, your wife still loves you."

"As if . . . there was. Any doubt," he said, rubbing my back in soft little circles.

Chapter 38

Life, Death, and the Gooey
Stuff In Between

Since things had gone better than expected with Grandma Jean, Dad decided to continue with his plan, which involved telling Uncle Jack and the Ice Queen about Grandpa Wade and the ball of light. Then they'd see Grandpa, and hopefully not freak out too badly.

Fenton and I had talked it over, and we agreed that the Ice Queen was the biggest risk. Grandma Jean and Uncle Jack could be trusted with family secrets, but the Ice Queen wasn't family, not yet. Even if she did love Dad, what was to keep her, after hearing the story and meeting Grandpa Wade, from driving to the newspaper in Red Lodge and handing them the news of the century? Blow the lid off our jar full of secrets and ruin everything.

The Ice Queen was due at one o'clock on Saturday, and Jack at four. Shortly before one I led Grandpa Wade into his room and said to stay there until we called for him.

"You 'n' Freddy [he meant Fenton] . . . don't like . . . Beverly," he said as he sat on his bed. "Why?"

"Actually, Grandpa, we pretty much hate her guts. Maybe if she wasn't dating Dad she'd be okay, but since she is dating him . . . Well, we wish she would move to Alaska and stay there. She's not our mom— it's as plain and simple as that. And if she marries Dad in August, the chance of Mom and Dad getting back together drops to zero."

Grandpa Wade thought for a moment. "Your father is . . . smart, caring man. If he chose Beverly . . . Well, maybe you and Freddy should . . . trust him? Give Beverly . . . some slack?"

I shrugged, not wanting to admit that he could be right, that Dad knew what he was doing when he asked the Ice Queen to marry him, and that *maybe* she had some good qualities, even if Fenton and I didn't see them.

Beverly showed up on time, holding a boxed apple pie she had bought at a bakery in Red Lodge. She greeted Dad by kissing him on the mouth, then said,

"Hello, children, how are you today?" to Fenton and me. I was so shocked that the Ice Queen was asking how we were doing, and without any snippiness in her voice, that I babbled like my tongue had suddenly fattened, while my brother squeaked out, "Fine." We didn't see that burst of humanity coming!

Dad and Beverly went into the kitchen so she could put the pie in the fridge, and Fenton and I dropped onto the couch and wrestled for the remote; the TV ban had been lifted, so we wanted to take advantage of it, but we couldn't agree on a program to watch. Though we were fighting, I still heard the Ice Queen say to Dad, "So what's the 'big story' you want to tell me? It doesn't involve us, does it? We're still okay?"

"We are more than okay," Dad said. "But there are some things you should know about my family, and my past."

"Family secrets? Should I be scared?"

"Not yet, but maybe soon," Dad said. I imagined the Ice Queen's look. It was an ugly, big-eyed and wild-haired, could-make-a-mirror-crack kind of look.

Dad called for Fenton and me to join them in the kitchen. But just as I turned off the TV, there was a pounding knock on the screen door.

There stood Sonny Baskins; beside him was a man

in his fifties who had the build of a gorilla. "Uh-oh," I said, grabbing Fenton's arm.

POUND! POUND! POUND!

"What's all the ruckus?" my dad said, going to the door. "Are you trying to knock my door off its hinges? And who's your friend?"

Sonny didn't answer. "Hand it over. Now!"

"Hand what over?" Dad asked. "What are you talking about?"

"I don't know what you are using, some kind of pill or potion or machine, but Tank and I are not leaving without it."

So the other guy was named Tank. *Great.*

The Ice Queen joined my father. "Who are these people?" she asked, but Sonny talked over her.

"First," he said, "your dead tree in the front yard magically comes alive again and grows *apples*, even though it's a maple tree. Next—"

"What is this man talking about?" Beverly asked Dad. To Sonny Baskins she said, "Are you on drugs or mentally unstable? Do I need to call 911?"

"Don't you dare call anyone," Sonny said. He yanked open the screen door, and he and Tank stepped inside our house. My grip on Fenton's arm grew stronger.

"Get out of my house!" Dad demanded of Sonny and Tank. "Or I'll call the cops."

"We'll leave when we are ready to leave," Sonny Baskins said. As his partner gave Fenton and me menacing looks, Sonny continued. "I happen to know that your dog, the mutt, was killed last year when he ran into a postal truck. But a few weeks ago I saw him, what was *left* of him, playing in the yard with the kids. Same with your father. Killed in a car crash a few years back, but the other day he was in your backyard, not dead at all."

He pulled a small plastic bag containing Grandpa Wade's broken-off toe from a pocket and held it near Dad's face. "Here's all the proof I need," Sonny said. "I believe this belongs to your father."

"You're crazy," Dad said, but he wasn't convincing. He's a big guy and might do okay if he had to fight Sonny Baskins. But if he also had to fight Tank, it was not going to end well for Dad.

"Whatever you own that can wake up dead things and people, give it to me right now," Sonny said. "Don't make me get violent—it's not my nature. But I will do whatever it takes to get possession of it. So hand it over!"

Now, here is where you might think, like I did, that maybe Sonny and Tank wanted to own the light ball so they could bring back dead relatives or pets they loved and missed, but no, that wasn't it. Sonny's next words, spoken in kind of a psycho blast, were, "I'm gonna sell it for a million dollars and move out of this stupid town!" That's right, it was all about money for Sonny and Tank. Greedy creeps!

And then—oh my God, I couldn't believe it!— Sonny pulled a handgun from under his shirt and pointed it right at my dad. "I'm not messing around here, Will. Give it to me—this minute!"

I froze. We were all about to be killed. I wanted to run. I wanted to scream. But I did none of that. That's the funny thing about fear. It gives you the strength to run ten miles in record time, but not always the push to get you started.

Surprisingly, the Ice Queen got that push! "No one points a gun at my fiancé," she cried, and snatched at the gun. She and Sonny Baskins struggled, and the gun went off. The noise was so loud my ears throbbed.

The Ice Queen—Beverly—fell to the floor. She had been shot in the stomach! She was bleeding like crazy: it gushed through her shirt and seeped down her shorts. I had never seen so much blood before.

"Damn it, no one was supposed to get hurt," Tank said. "I'm out of here." He hurried out the door.

"Hey, where are you going?" Sonny shouted, then he dashed after Tank. They scuttled across our front yard toward Sonny's property. Seconds later I heard Sonny's truck start up.

I let go of Fenton's arm and ran to Beverly. Dad was crouched over her, holding her hand and pleading that she stick around—"Don't leave me! Stay right here!"—but the bullet had done too much damage. Beverly looked at Dad and smiled at Fenton and me in what seemed like a warm and genuine way, then her eyelids fluttered and she died.

"Dear God in heaven!" Dad cried. He frantically checked Beverly's wrists for a pulse, and then he put an ear to her chest. "No!" he shrieked. "Please! No!"

The Ice Queen died trying to save us from being shot by Sonny Baskins. Doesn't that make her a hero? Sometimes you think you know someone, have them categorized as good or bad or mean or friendly, but then one day they do something so unexpected you realize that you don't know them at all.

"I'll call 911," Fenton said, running to the phone.

"Yes, hurry!" Dad said, but then he changed his mind. "Wait," he told Fenton. "It's too late for that— she's dead. What we need is the lightning ball. Go get it!"

I don't think I've ever moved so fast in my life. Back in the living room, I twisted off the lid, but this time the light ball did not instantly leap out and go to work. I shook the jar and smacked the glass, but I couldn't get it to leave the jar.

"Come on," I said to the light. "Do your stuff. Now!"

Finally the great ball of light jumped out of the jar, landed on the Ice Queen's chest, and dove inside and filled her with light—some of it shot right out of the bullet hole in her stomach; it creepily looked like she was leaking light. As Dad, Fenton, and I watched with hope and worry and twelve other emotions jammed together in a tangled mess, the ball rose up out of her body and settled into the jar. I twisted on the lid, and we waited for some kind of change.

"Please work," Dad said, smacking his hands together in a clumsy clap. His cheeks were soaked with tears. For him alone I wished that the Ice Queen would return and be just like how she used to be, no matter what Fenton and I thought about her, or what she thought about us. None of that little stuff mattered anymore.

Another minute or two ticked away, and nothing seemed to be happening with Beverly. Had the light ball failed to launch life? I wondered.

But then I noticed that blood was no longer pouring out of Beverly's belly. Just as I was about to say something to Dad, Bev opened her eyes, giving all of us a jolt, and looked around like she was unsure what world she was in.

"It worked!" Dad cried. "Oh yes, it worked!" He placed a thumb on Beverly's right wrist, but his troubled look told me he couldn't find a pulse. He then tried her chest and neck, but he didn't find what he was looking for, proof of life. It looked like Dad was in danger of losing it, but his undead girlfriend started talking, and that seemed to calm him down a little.

"What happened?" the Ice Queen blearily asked. "Did I pass out?"

"Uh, yes, in a way you did pass out," Dad said. He exhaled hard and helped Beverly sit up. She saw all the blood on her shirt and shorts and the rug and gasped.

"My God! What is wrong with me?" she said. "There's so much blood!"

Five seconds of terrible silence.

"You were, how can I say this . . . accidentally shot by our neighbor," Dad said. "Or maybe it wasn't an accident—I don't really know. But now you are back with us, as good as new." He put on a smile he couldn't keep going long.

"But how . . . or what? I don't get it," Beverly said, glancing at the bullet wound and looking away—it was a horrible sight. "If I lost all that blood, how can I be alive? That makes no sense!"

Dad looked frantically at Fenton and me—how could he explain all this? He then gripped Bev's arm. "Technically—now don't panic, okay, sweetie? Technically, you aren't alive. It's kind of a strange story."

"Will, what on earth are you talking about?" she said, fear in her voice—and in her eyes, too. "I'm not . . . alive? Is that what you are *really* trying to tell me?"

My dad sighed miserably and nodded at me. I held up the light ball for Beverly to see. She blinked several times—maybe it was too bright for her zombie eyes. "I don't get it. What is that weird thing?"

"A light ball, actually. It's been performing miracles for my family since I was a kid," Dad said. "That was one of the things I had planned to tell you today, before things got . . . off track."

Off track?—that was something that happened to slot cars and toy trains. This was off the charts!

"As it turns out, darling, you're the latest miracle," Dad said to the Ice Queen. "You were shot in the stomach, and then you sort of, well, I'll just say it . . . died. But the lightning ball brought you back, though not quite all the way." He took her hand, nodding like a madman, as if his nodding would make it all believable to her. "Crazy, isn't it, that something like this could happen in real life?" he finished.

Beverly looked at my dad for the longest time, like she was waiting for him to say *Just kidding!* She was a nurse and probably hadn't seen many miracles of the life-and-death kind, surely nothing involving a resurrection caused by a ball of light.

When no such words came from Dad, fear and disbelief returned to Beverly's face. She put a thumb to her wrist, and then a hand on her neck by the big artery, hunting for a pulse she was not going to find.

"Not possible," she said. She did a second round of pulse searching, then groaned as the realization that she was in fact a dead person settled in. Her eyes got a glazed look to them. It was a scary look, and I was worried about what she might do next. Just because Grandpa Wade wasn't violent when we woke him up, that didn't mean the same would be true with other dead people pulled back to life.

"I know this has to be difficult for you," Dad said. "But . . . we'll figure it out together. One minute and then one hour and then one day at a time."

"No!" Bev said, fire showing up in her eyes. "No . . .

NO!" She pulled her hand away from Dad and started to shake, like a full body tremble—that was also scary. "I do NOT accept any of this. NO!"

"But . . . but . . ." Dad had run out of words. He looked like a wrecked man.

I glanced at Fenton. He shook his head at me, so I matched it by throwing up my arms. This was new territory, and none of us, including Beverly, knew what to expect. But I will say this: I did feel bad for the Ice Queen. She may not have been the sunniest person when alive, but now that she was undead . . . Well, she was not anywhere close to being happy.

Beverly began sobbing, was probably using up the last of her teardrop supply.

"So how is this supposed to work, being a dead person?" she asked at last. "I can't go out in the world, can I? Won't people be able to tell that I'm messed up?"

"You can stay here with us," Dad said, running a hand through his sweaty hair. "Turns out, we have some experience sheltering the undead."

As if on cue Grandpa Wade appeared, shuffling into the living room with the help of his walking stick. He saw Beverly, the big splotches of blood on her clothing and the carpet, and the light ball, and figured out what had happened right away.

"I'm Wade," he said to her. "Will's father . . . kid's grandpa. You must be Beverly. Nice to . . . meet you. Sorry didn't happen. More ideal circum-stances."

Beverly stared at Grandpa Wade, looking like she was about to be ill. "You're a dead guy, right? That's so great!"

"Prefer term 'undead,'" Grandpa said. "Takes away . . . sting."

Dad, Fenton, and I looked from one to the other uneasily, and Grandpa Wade didn't seem to know what to do with himself—stay or go? Bev then reached for a cabinet handle and pulled herself up. Dad went to help her, but a spitty hiss from his fiancée caused him to keep his distance.

Standing, the Ice Queen hacked and wheezed like she was trying to force herself to breathe. *A rookie error*, Grandpa might have been thinking—the undead have no need for oxygen. Next, Beverly lifted the tails of her bloody blouse and inspected the damage to her stomach. She dropped the f-bomb, and then she dropped her shirt.

"Not acceptable," she said kind of quietly, but then her next words were said louder. "I can't . . . I just can't live like this. I won't!" She put a hand against her stomach and hurried to the door.

"Where are you going?" Dad asked as Bev pushed open the screen door, but the question did not stop her—she headed straight to her car. Inside it, she smacked the steering wheel, flipped us the double bird as we gathered on the porch, and then backed down the driveway and headed up the road, gunning it and kicking up gravel.

"This is an absolute nightmare," Dad said, kind of summing things up. I leaned against him so he knew he was not dealing with all of this by himself.

"Not sure . . . driving while undead. A good idea," Grandpa Wade said, which made me wonder whether he and dad were worried about what *I* was worried about, that the Ice Queen might do something stupid like crash her car into a tree with the hope of restoring her deadness.

"I should probably go after her," Dad said as we watched Beverly's car until it was gone from view. "Where's she going in such a big hurry?"

He patted his pockets to make sure he had his car keys and took a few steps toward his SUV, but then a realization, or something, caused him to change course. He looked over at Sonny's property.

"On second thought, we better get out of here, all of us, in case Sonny and his friend return," he said, blinking his eyes as a way of ridding them of tears, I guess. Dad then glanced at the barrel jar as I clutched it to my chest. "The first thing we need to do is get rid of the lightning ball, right now. It's done enough damage to this family."

"And some good things too," I protested, but Dad stepped past me and went inside.

"We're leaving in two minutes," he said.

Five minutes later—everyone except Grandpa Wade needed to use the bathroom first, and Dad twice tried calling Bev's cell phone, but it was off, apparently—Dad and Grandpa and Fenton and I were in Dad's car; I was shaking but managed to keep hold of the jar. Fenton then remembered Scruffy, so he ran to the storm cellar, tore open the doors, picked up the hellhound, and carried him to the car.

"I don't want Mr. Baskins coming back and finding Scruffy and hurting him," he explained, climbing into the backseat. Scruffy was agitated, he hadn't gone for a car ride since he had been alive, so Fenton handed him off to Grandpa Wade for a selfish, yet practical, reason: if Scruffy bit Grandpa Wade there'd be no pain or blood.

"Where are we going?" I asked as Dad screeched down the driveway.

"The Beartooth Mountains," he said. "We'll take the lightning ball as high up the mountain as we can get by foot and set it free. And maybe we can go back to living normal lives again."

We were about a quarter mile down the road when Fenton said, "Dad? What if the Ice . . . What if Beverly goes to the cops and tells them everything? Or to the hospital for treatment and they figure out she's dead? Or undead, I mean."

"Or she could go to the newspaper and blab everything," I added.

Dad looked at us in the rearview mirror. "Guys? Those are good questions, but let's just deal with the light ball right now, get rid of it, and then, well, whatever happens happens, okay?"

Fenton and I nodded. In my head I had a vision of everything blowing up. The cops were going to pull us over and take us and the light ball into custody. And then they'd hand us over to some little-known government agency, and we'd disappear from the world. Years from now people in Deerwood and Red Lodge would still be talking about the North family, and how they vanished on a summer day. One of the greatest mysteries to ever haunt southern Montana.

Just in case our lives were about to blow up, there

were some things I wanted to say while there was time. To the great ball of light I silently said that I wasn't mad at it, even though it had drawn an angry Sonny Baskins into our lives and resurrected the Ice Queen against her wishes. *You always did your best for us*, I said in my thoughts. *Thank you.*

And then to Grandpa Wade I said, "Hey, Grandpa, thanks for saving Dad's life when he was a kid. You know, when you asked God for help after the tractor accident. Fenton and I probably wouldn't be here if you hadn't done that. So thanks tons." I couldn't hug him from the backseat so I squeezed his shoulder.

"Oh—you're welcome, Fiona," he said. "That's what . . . families do. Save each other."

Dad and Grandpa Wade exchanged a warm look that told me at least *one* problem was a problem no longer. And, after all, wasn't that our goal in the first place? Now all we had to do was survive Sonny Baskins (and possibly Tank) and his evil plans, figure out how to keep Beverly from spilling the beans about her death and reboot, avoid cops, government agents, and reporters, and then *maybe* we'd have a chance to be a happy family.

Chapter 39

The Beartooth Mountains

A minute later we saw Sonny Baskins's old truck idling on an intersecting road, near the stop sign. Just Sonny was in there, it looked like—there was no sign of Tank.

"Crud!" Dad said, pushing down on the gas pedal. "It's like he was waiting for us to drive by. Why did I come this way? Stupid!"

It didn't take long before Sonny and his truck were seeable in the mirrors. Dad drove even faster, which was about the only option. Because we lived in farm country there weren't many side roads or turnoffs or places to hide.

"Dad?" I said, my heart racing. "What if Mr. Baskins catches us?"

"I won't let him hurt you guys," he said, with a shaky kind of confidence. "And I won't let him take the light ball. Who knows what he'd do with it if he got his hands on it."

Even though I hate guns (except BB guns, air rifles, potato guns, and water pistols), I wished that Dad owned a shotgun that we could use to scare off Sonny Baskins, so we'd have a better chance of making it through the day alive. In case Sonny started shooting at our car, I slid down in my seat and motioned to Fenton to do the same. *Don't let him hurt us*, I asked of God, in case he was watching the events unfold.

We were about ten minutes into our escape when it started to rain, so Dad turned on the windshield wipers. I looked ahead and saw a sky overtaken by dark ominous clouds; we were heading into a storm. I then peeked through the rear window. Sonny's truck was getting closer. A second storm was trailing us.

"Can you go any faster?" Fenton asked our father. "He's almost on us!"

"I can't go much faster without risking an accident," Dad said. I checked the speedometer—he was driving at eighty miles per hour, passing cars and trucks when they got in the way.

I looked at the ball of light resting on my lap. *Please save us one more time*, I said to it with my thoughts. *One more favor before we send you away.*

The rain fell harder and I heard thunder. I thought about my mother, probably in her Manhattan apartment, completely unaware that her kids and ex-husband were in danger. I felt a blaze of fury toward her. If she hadn't left us, maybe none of this would have happened.

As we passed south of Red Lodge on the Beartooth Highway, Dad found his cell phone and said he was thinking of calling the cops and asking for help, that we might have reached a point where keeping our secrets was more of a danger than telling them would be.

But he couldn't get reception. Typical. The mountains blocked the signals. That was the only reason Fenton and I hadn't bugged Dad for cell phones. It would be dumb owning something that almost never worked.

The rain beat down, but I could see the mountains up ahead, and the Gallatin National Forest, which is connected to Yellowstone National Park, though nearly all of Yellowstone is in Wyoming.

We had been to Gallatin four or five times, so I expected Dad to enter it through the main entrance. Instead he drove past it and searched for a fire road.

I looked back. I didn't see Sonny's truck, though I couldn't see very far because of the rain.

"I think we lost him," I said.

"I hope so," Dad said. "But to be safe, let's assume that he's still chasing us."

He found a fire road and we drove up it—it wouldn't take us all the way to the mountains, but it was more of a direct route than the main road. It was unpaved, and the car was sliding on mud and grass, but then Dad flipped a switch that allowed for four-wheel drive and we got better traction.

Meanwhile the storm was getting nastier, the lightning flashing constantly, and we were driving into its heart as the fire road took us closer to the mountains and to Granite Peak, the highest point in Montana.

We drove for about a mile before we were stopped by a low wooden fence and by a sign saying that vehicles were not permitted beyond that point. If Sonny Baskins had been on our tail I think Dad would have plowed through the fence and kept going, but since he wasn't, Dad stopped the car and turned off the engine.

The plan, he said, was for us to run to the base of the mountains, about three hundred yards away, release the light ball, and hope that it didn't follow us back to the car. He glanced at Grandpa Wade. "Do you mind staying behind with Scruffy? Not to be rude, but you guys might slow us down a bit."

"No problem," he said. "Scruffy 'n' I . . . man fort."

It didn't go as planned. As soon as Dad opened his door, Scruffy leaped out of the car and ran off. Fenton and I dashed after him, calling and calling, but we couldn't see him anywhere.

"Let's worry about Scruffy later," Dad yelled out to us. "First, let's ditch the light ball."

Soaked to the bone already, we climbed over the fence and were just breaking into a run toward the mountains when we heard a vehicle coming up the fire road! My mind raced—what would be worse, a park ranger or Sonny Baskins? We were going to find out—it was Sonny's red truck. He parked next to Dad's car, jumped out, and strode toward us.

"What do you have in that jar, Fiona?" he asked, posting a smile that was as fake as a three-dollar bill. "I'd like to take a look at it if you don't mind."

"Forget it," I said, walking backward. "It's not meant for the likes of you."

Sonny dropped his smile. "Hand it over and no one else will get hurt. I got nothing to lose here. So give it to me!"

"Why don't you get back in your truck and get out

of here and leave us alone," Dad said to Sonny Baskins.

"Sure," he said. "As soon as you give me whatever is in that jar. Now!"

I felt the great ball of light pulsing faster than usual. Was it as frightened as I was?

When Sonny stepped closer, Dad yelled, "Run!" So we ran through the rain, thunder booming above us and lightning flashing near the mountains. I pressed the barrel jar to my chest. No way was I letting Sonny Baskins get it.

We were running hard, but Sonny was gaining ground—for an old guy he was going at a pretty good clip.

"Get back here, Fiona, so we can get this matter settled," he bellowed. I turned to see him sliding his hand under his shirt like he was going for his gun.

A super huge "No thanks!" from me as I ran as fast as my legs could go, but still Sonny was nearly on us. Then an other-worldly squealing sound pierced through the thunder. Scruffy! My dog came

Get back here, FIONA!

dashing from our left and leaped at Sonny, knocking him to the ground. He bit and snapped at Sonny's legs and arms as Sonny tried to fight him off.

"Go, Scruffy!" I yelled. An old instinct to protect his family had kicked in, and my undead dog was risking his second life to save us from harm. Even in death Scruffy turned out to be loyal. It was a sweet surprise.

Dad shouted for Fenton and me to keep running, so I lost sight of what was happening with Sonny and Scruffy. When we were about a hundred feet from the mountains, lightning crackling all around us and nearly scaring me out of my sneakers, I tripped over a branch, fell, and lost hold of the barrel jar. It smashed against a rock and cracked into a dozen jagged pieces.

Fenton and Dad stopped running and moved closer to me and to the ball of light. The ball just sat there

for a moment, like it was deciding what to do, and then it bounced away from the broken glass like a basketball being dribbled a foot off the ground.

I stood up and something amazing happened. The great ball of light bounced one more time then shot through my stomach, giving me a case of the cosmic tingles, and came out the other side near the base of my spine. It then circled above Dad, Fenton, and me like it was saying good-bye, and zipped toward the clouds and merged with a huge lightning bolt flashing across the sky.

"Good-bye, and thanks for everything," I said to the light ball. "Go help some other people if you can." Maybe it would return to Earth one day, and maybe it would stay heaven-bound. I wasn't sure which way it would go.

And then a jolt of worry struck: What if Grandpa Wade had just died again, back in the car? Now that the light was gone, there was no way to even try a second dose. *So please don't die again, Grandpa.*

As rain fell and thunder growled, Fenton gave me a worried look, and Dad gripped my shoulder and asked if I was feeling okay, seeing as how the light ball had just passed through me.

"I'm fine," I said, though in truth I was feeling kind of strange, like my cells had been electrified. I also

felt a little airy in my sneakers, like at any moment I might shoot up to the clouds like the light ball had. "I just want to go home," I said.

"Hopefully, we'll be home soon," Dad said. "But first we better find out what's going on with Sonny Baskins. If he broke free of Scruffy and is coming after us, let's run west along the base of the mountain. I think the ranger station is that way."

We cautiously crept back to our car, on the lookout for Sonny and Scruffy. But when we reached the spot where they had been tussling, there was no sign of them. Since Sonny's truck was where he had parked it, two possibilities came to mind: Sonny had run off and Scruffy ran after him; or, less likely, Scruffy had killed or injured Sonny and dragged him off somewhere.

As Fenton and Dad and I searched the grass for Sonny's handgun without luck, Grandpa Wade came up to us clutching a tire iron. Dad asked Grandpa Wade if he saw what had happened with Sonny and Scruffy. Grandpa's slow-moving answer was that he had seen a bit of the struggle, but then the rain had gotten too heavy to see more than about a foot ahead. When the rain thinned and he could have seen them again, Sonny and Scruffy were gone.

"Was gonna pop Sonny . . . with tire iron," he said.

"Never liked him. Think he . . . has hedge clippers. Lent him. Ten years ago."

I wanted to launch a search for Scruffy, but Dad said that with Sonny Baskins out there somewhere it was too risky. Plus he was worried that if we stuck around much longer, a ranger would show up and ask questions.

As we climbed into the SUV, I panoramically scanned the forest and the mountains, hoping to see Scruffy, but it didn't happen. And then I checked the sky, hoping to see the great ball of light zipping across storm clouds as they rolled east, but that didn't happen either. I owed my life to my dog for pouncing on Sonny Baskins before he could pull out his gun and shoot me, and to the light ball for saving Dad so I could be born. But I suspected that I would never see either of them again.

Waterlogged and weary but happy to be alive, I fastened my seat belt. Dad started the engine, turned around, and headed for the road.

"It's done," Dad said to Grandpa Wade. "We are free of the lightning ball, and it is free of us."

"As it . . . should be," Grandpa Wade said.

I hoped, but was unsure, that we had done the right thing by freeing the light ball. Another question that might never find an answer.

* Chapter 10 *

Vacation Time

We drove home, but only stayed long enough to change out of our wet clothes, pack clothing and camping gear into Dad's car, and clean up the blood Beverly had spilled in the living room, including splashing bleach on the carpet. Dad had decided that it wasn't safe for us to stay at the farm until further notice. If Sonny was alive he could still be gunning for us, and there was a chance his friend Tank could reappear at any time.

Dad's other worry—a second reason we needed to leave town—was that the Ice Queen was unstable and he didn't know what to expect from her, including whether she would reveal to friends or strangers that she had been shot and was now a zombie, and soon thousands of people would invade our farm, trying to get their hands on the ball of light, and reporters would hound us night and day, trying to get to the truth.

"Apparently, she hasn't gone to the police yet, but . . . Well, who knows what she might ultimately do," Dad said to Grandpa Wade as we loaded junk into the SUV. "Whatever that thing is, it could cause a serious disruption, or threat, to our lives. It might be best for all of us if we aren't too easy to find for a while." He looked really upset about the whole thing. So much for his big wedding plans.

Inside my head I had a creepy thought that I wasn't planning to share, but if you made it this far I'm guessing that you might be okay with a certain amount of creepiness. So here it is. Remember, shortly after we brought back Scruffy, how he dug at his grave near the outbuilding like he wanted to go back there to live? That was what I saw in my head, Beverly digging a grave with a shovel, sliding inside it, pulling the dirt down on top of her, and staying there until the recharge the light ball provided wore off, and then for all of eternity after that. I told you it was creepy. You were warned!

Before we left, Dad called the Ice Queen's cell

phone and home phone, but she didn't answer. On her home phone he left a message saying that even if she was still mad and never wanted to see him again, could she at least send a text saying she was okay?

"Maybe I screwed up by bringing you back to the world without your okay," Dad said to the machine. "But the intention behind it was good. Oh well, good-bye, Bev. It was fun." When he hung up, it seemed like he was trying to keep his emotions on lockdown for the benefit of the rest of us. We needed to stay focused on getting out of town ASAP.

But before we did that, Dad phoned Uncle Jack and told him to not show up for the barbecue, since we had decided to take a vacation and wouldn't be there. He asked Jack to find someone to take care of the animals while we were away, and Jack promised to do that. Dad didn't say anything about what had happened to the Ice Queen or that Sonny Baskins might still have it in for us, which I thought might be a little risky for whoever was going to be tending to the animals. Dad also didn't tell Uncle Jack about Grandpa Wade being undead—it was not really something you could say over the phone. I suppose my uncle will find out the shocking truth soon enough.

Dad locked up the house, and we piled into the car

and drove away from Bluebird Acres, heading east. Dad had put together a vacation plan where we would spend two weeks or so in the Dakotas seeing roadside attractions such as the world's largest garden gnome, and we'd stay at campgrounds and small-town motels. He and Grandpa Wade had decided against inviting Grandma Jean along for the trip so as to not put her at risk should Sonny or Tank find us, or should a different danger arise if someone figured out that we were transporting a zombie. Grandpa Wade was upset about being separated from Grandma Jean again, but he was excited about the vacation. He had spent his entire life and all his death in a narrow section of Montana, but now he was finally getting the chance to see a bit of our country.

The farther we traveled away from my house, the more I was becoming a basket case. First, we were checking the mirrors every minute in case Sonny Baskins was hot on our trail. As Dad explained it, even if we could convince Sonny that we no longer owned the light ball, it did not mean we were off the hook. We had seen him shoot and kill Beverly, and what if he wanted to get rid of the witnesses so we couldn't report him to the police?

Second, I was still worried that Grandpa Wade could croak at any moment, and now that the ball of light was gone there was no way for us to even try to bring him back.

Third, the feeling that I would not see my home or town for a long time was growing stronger. Maybe I was being silly, but I could not shake the belief that some great things were ending, without a new thing arriving to fill in the empty space. It was like with every mile that we drove we passed through a turnstile, the kind that lets you go forward, but if you changed your mind and tried to turn around it wouldn't let you. Forward was the only option, even if you didn't want it to be.

I loved Bluebird Acres. I didn't want to be away from it for weeks or months or years.

We were somewhere west of Billings when I asked Dad if we should phone Mom in New York and tell her about our vacation plans. "Maybe she'll want to join us in the Dakotas," I said, trying to sound more hopeful than I was feeling.

There was about a half minute of silence, then Dad pointed out in his being-nice voice that Fenton's and my mother probably had a busy work and social schedule planned for the next few weeks and wouldn't be able to slip away, even for a day or two. There would also be the little matter of explaining the return of Grandpa Wade without her "busting a valve."

"It was a good idea, Fiona," he said, catching my reflection in the rearview mirror, "but you know how your mother is. She doesn't do well with surprises or spur-of-the-moment plans, or with things that don't fit neatly into her worldview. I'm sorry. I wish your mother was more like the rest of us, I guess."

Yes, I did know how my mother was, unfortunately. The last time Fenton and I had visited her in New York, on our first night there she yelled at a taxi driver for making us wait outside her building for two minutes, then later at a snazzy restaurant she gave the maître d', our waiter, and a busboy a hard time for what she considered to be bad service. She had become a snoot, the kind of person who thinks that just about everyone in the world except for herself and her circle of friends isn't up to snuff. She used to be a little bit that way when she lived with us in Montana, but it was like New York City brought out the worst in her and helped her perfect those faults.

Sadly, Dad was right about Mom. No matter what we said to her, or how passionately Fenton and I pleaded, she was not going to be joining us on our vacation. It really stinks when asking your mother to come see you when you run into some trouble is not a realistic option.

My family and I continued traveling east. Grandpa Wade grabbed a book, *Moby Dick* by Herman Melville, and began reading it. I haven't read that novel yet, but I'm rooting for the whale. When it's man versus nature, I'm usually on the side of nature. Does that make me a traitor to my species?

Second Chances, Second Choices

I would love to tell you that after the great ball of light passed through me at Gallatin National Forest, I suddenly had superhero powers, that I could fly above the trees and shoot lasers out of my eyes and flames out of my butt. No such luck.

But the light ball did leave something behind.

Call it a seed, or a kernel of some kind, that, under the right conditions, might one day sprout beautiful flowers.

Or maybe it's more like an idea, a possibility.

I think it has something to do with second chances and the choices we make.

And there is something in there about new beginnings, not just after death, but right here, right now, in the living world.

I've been thinking a lot about the ball of light and the miracles it caused.

When it first appeared, the day of the tractor accident, my dad and grandpa were given a second chance. My father was allowed to continue with his life—real life, not the zombie kind—and Grandpa Wade was given a chance to be a better father and husband. I would bet that for a long while after the accident there was no better dad in all of Montana, and that Grandpa Wade believed the light ball had saved two people that day. Eventually he went back to being a drunk and a lousy dad and husband, but that was his choice, to start drinking again. The light ball didn't make any demands. It caused the miracle and let those affected by it take it from there.

And then when Fenton and I used the light ball to wake up Grandpa Wade he took advantage of his last chance and became a better father, husband, and grandpa, and a bit of a book nut. He could be a big grump if he wanted to be, but he decided to reach for something better.

When the dead maple tree was given a second chance it chose to be an apple tree. Yes, I'm saying that the maple tree made a choice. That's part of the second-chance deal the light ball provides. Here you are again, so what do you want to do?

With Scruffy, given a second life, he decided that he'd rather be a hellhound than a playful pup. Maybe during his first life he'd looked at Dobermans with envy, and wondered why he couldn't be an alpha dog. When the light woke him up he finally had his chance to join that team.

Which brings me to the curious case of the Ice Queen.

Instead of jumping at the opportunity to have a second life and a second chance, after Beverly was killed by a gunshot and then awoken by the light ball she became angry at my dad for bringing her back without her permission, and upset that her old life as a nurse and a neighbor and everything else she was had been wiped out since she could no longer pass for a living person. No gratitude for what the great ball of light had done for her, and no appreciation for the rare miracle of a second life. But plenty of grumbling and finger pointing, that was for sure.

This one puzzled me for a long time. In every other case (except for maybe Mercury the mouse) the ball of light had done good things. It even gave tiny feet to a worm so it could get around better. But with the Ice Queen it brought back a woman who was not a happy camper, and who, if we believed her words, would rather be dead than undead.

How could something that restores life allow such misery and anger? I wondered. Wasn't the light ball supposed to be all about love and healing and second chances?

Then it hit me—free will and free choices. The light ball does not judge, or nudge. It simply awakens dead things, maybe with a *hope* of a happy ending, but whether that happens or not is up to whomever or whatever was brought back. In the Ice Queen's case she chose in her second life to not be much different from how she was in her first life—difficult to deal with! Maybe that had something to do with the fact that she had only been dead for a few minutes before the light ball woke her up. It's only a guess, but maybe if she had been dead for a long while before returning, she would have had greater appreciation for the zombie life and the absolute miracle of post-death bonus days.

Or not. I cannot honestly say I have a great understanding of what the Ice Queen is all about. Living or dead.

All this rambling leads to my biggest scientific conclusion yet: free will is not lost, even if someone dies and is given a second life. And it's the same kind of free will we have in this life.

So, even though I'd love to live in a perfect world where everyone is always nice to each other, I think there will always be good people and bad people, and selfless people and selfish people, and it's up to us to decide what kind of person we want to be. Because we have free will, one of God's greatest gifts to people (and to dogs, trees, and possibly worms).

And now I need to rest my brain. It's been running way beyond its usual capacity. Red warning lights are flashing!

Chapter 12

Where Do We Go from Here?

This is our fifth day of travel. We are currently in southern North Dakota, and if the lousy weather breaks we should be in northern South Dakota sometime tomorrow. (That sentence looks funny on paper. All those norths and souths squished together.)

So far there has been no sign of Sonny Baskins or his friend Tank, and there's a good chance that neither one of them is chasing us. Two days ago Dad checked the Internet on his phone and found an article in the *Carbon County News* saying that Sonny's truck had been found at Gallatin National Forest, but there was no sign of Sonny, so rangers and a mountain rescue team have been searching for him.

I know I should be nice and hope that Sonny is

found alive and healthy, but that's a hope I have trouble holding on to for long. If he is alive, Sonny could be lost in the millions of acres that are Gallatin National Forest and Yellowstone. If he's dead, that could be Scruffy's fault. Or maybe a grizzly bear killed him. Stuff like that happens in the wild all the time. Bears need to eat too, right?

In other news, Dad had been calling the Ice Queen two or three times each day, hoping that she was okay and less upset than when we last saw her in Deerwood. He finally reached her last night while we were staying at a campground near a town called Napoleon. After he hung up, Dad told Grandpa Wade and Fenton and me that Beverly had decided to move to one of the Indian reservations in Montana, both to hide out and to provide free nursing services to poor Native Americans until "death caught up to her." Dad's grim look told me he was hoping for some words from the Ice Queen such as "I forgive you" that never showed up.

So I guess a second shot at life didn't turn the Ice Queen into Beverly Sunshine, dispenser of happiness, hugs, and soothing words. But at least she was planning to do some good by helping people in need of nursing. Good for her. I truly hope she enjoys whatever time the light ball gave to her. If I (with Fenton's help!) made her first life more difficult than it needed to be, well, I'm sorry. I know that I'm too quick to judge people, and not just Dad's girlfriends. That's one thing I need to work on.

Anyway.

We are all much calmer than the day we left Bluebird Acres, though we might not be out of the woods yet. Even if no one is chasing us, what if a park ranger finds Scruffy and Sonny Baskins (or what is left of Sonny) and connects them to us?

Or what if a sharp-eyed Native American man or woman realizes that the new nurse on the reservation—the Ice Queen—is a zombie and calls the FBI, and then Beverly tells the FBI agents the entire story? That could be bad, especially for Grandpa Wade. Would the government take him away so they could conduct experiments? And would Dad, Fenton, and I have to join the Witness Protection Program and change our names and move somewhere so the crazies leave us alone?

Grandpa Wade has gotten plenty of funny looks whenever we stop at gas stations and restaurants and campgrounds and motels, but so far no one has accused him of being undead. The closest we came to trouble was when the sweaty owner of a motel we stayed at in eastern Montana on our first night of travel looked closely at Grandpa Wade, and then pulled Dad aside and asked if his father was feeling okay. Dad explained that Wade had been in a car accident, which was why he looked like "death warmed over." I'm pretty sure the man didn't believe Dad, but he rented two rooms to us and left us alone.

While we were at the motel I borrowed Dad's phone so I could check my email, which I mostly used for school stuff. There was only one email, from my science teacher, Mr. Embry. I don't think he'd mind if I shared it with you.

Dear Fiona:

I was going to stop by your house and have a chat with you and your father about the "apple" you gave me on the last day of school, but instead I decided to put my thoughts down on paper. Or rather e-paper!

I had never seen an apple like the one you gave to me, so I sent it to a friend who is an expert on fruit trees. He ran some tests and declared that the specimen was a hybrid fruit produced by a tree that was part apple tree and part maple tree. What's more, the species of apple tree that was half of the biological equation is not known to exist anywhere on Earth, and he checked every possible database.

Naturally, we were excited about the "discovery." It's not often that we as men of science come across something new. One reason I wanted to talk with your father was to find out if he had been grafting different kinds of trees together, and if so, I'd want to know where he had obtained the apple specimen.

But then I thought about why you gave the apple to me. Was it simply for me to determine the chemical components that made up the apple? Or did you have a bigger reason in mind?

I went with "bigger reason"! In doing so I sent myself back to my childhood when my love of science first took root. It seemed like the entire world was ripe for exploring, whether it involved cataloging insects I found in my backyard, or charting the stars above me.

Many years later I became a science teacher at Roosevelt Middle School, a job I love, especially when it comes to dealing with eager minds like the one you possess. But it's fair to say I became lazy. I taught the same classes year after year, and even used the same lesson plans and books. It was like I had forgotten the reason I became a scientist, which was to be an explorer and researcher, and maybe someday write a book about my experiences.

What it took to remind me of my love for science and my plans for the future was the tiny apple you gave me as a gift. But the true gift was the rediscovery of something I used to think I would never lose, that push to learn everything I can about the majestic world we live in. And now that love for science has returned. Thank you so much for that gift.

What this means is that I'm taking a leave of absence from my teaching job, and joining a team of scientists planning to explore a small section of the Amazon rain forest, where we will catalog all forms of life that we find there. If you are interested I will send you occasional updates and photos. I owe you that much. You helped free me from my laziness. Thank you, Fiona, for everything you and a certain apple have done for me.

Your friend in science and in life,

Greg Embry

Just some words from my favorite teacher, but they set off a fountain of tears. The great ball of light was still causing second chances and new beginnings, even though it might be circling Venus for all I know.

•••

Tonight we are staying at a motel in North Dakota that is home to the largest statue of a great blue heron in the world. The sucker is forty feet tall and made of steel, and it's set in front of the motel near the highway. Why anyone would want to build a giant metal bird I do not know, but there it is, in its freakish glory.

Other roadside attractions we have seen include the world's largest cow statue, the world's largest fake catfish, and a huge statue of a turtle riding a snowmobile. We have not yet seen the world's largest garden gnome, since Dad found out it's in Canada, and I couldn't talk him into driving us up there just to see a giant gnome.

Fenton and I are staying in room 6, and Dad and Grandpa Wade are next door in room 7. It's late, well past midnight. Fenton has been asleep for an hour, but I stayed awake so I could write this story, not sure if anyone will believe it, but wanting to get it down on paper anyway.

It's been raining all day. Hearing thunder rumble, I set down my pen and notebook and go to the window, but there's not much to see, and I'm pointed in the wrong direction for seeing an approaching storm—east.

So I leave the room and stand underneath an

overhang and watch raindrops smack into trees and cars. Lightning then explodes across the sky, knocking out light-sensitive streetlamps set along the highway, and lighting up the statue of the heron, which is kind of an eerie sight.

There's a rattling thunder boom, followed by more lightning flashes. Weirdly, I get that tingly feeling inside my stomach like I used to get when the great ball of light was near and trying to communicate with me. But the last time I saw the light ball it was shooting up to the sky above Gallatin National Forest, so there's no way it could be close.

Unless . . .

Is it possible that the light ball followed us to North Dakota, like maybe it's not done messing with us in good and bad and freaky ways? Probably not, since the belly butterflies just vanished. It was a fun thought, though, imagining the light ball returning and what experiments Fenton and I might conduct. (So many cemeteries, so little time.)

Anyway.

I guess I should go back to my room and work on my book. Then, if I'm not too sleepy, I'm going to write a letter to my mother and tell her everything that has happened these past several weeks, and finally

say how I feel about her running away, which, on one hand, I can respect in a putting-her-free-will-to-use kind of way, but on the other hand it completely sucks and seems beyond selfish. Hey lady, you have a husband and two kids. Hello?

So you could say I will use my free will—choosing to write the letter—to question my mother's use of her free will to run away. Maybe in the letter I will point out some helpful examples of how others have used their free will to become better people, including Grandpa Wade, who decided in his second go-round to be a good grandpa and dad. Perhaps I'll even mention the Ice Queen's decision to provide nursing services to Native Americans, something she might not have ever done if she hadn't died and been brought back.

Hmm. I'm kind of scared about what might happen— or worse, not happen—after my mother reads the letter, and that I'm setting myself up for another huge disappointment. I'm excited, too, about the possibilities. But mostly I'm scared.

So that's it for now. Good night, reader. Thanks so much for sticking around. You were magnificent!

Did you LOVE reading this book?

Visit the Whyville...

Where you can:

- ◇ Discover great books!
- ◇ Meet new friends!
- ◇ Read exclusive sneak peeks and more!

Log on to visit now!
bookhive.whyville.net

Two **wildly original** *adventures from Evan Kuhlman*

atheneum

From Atheneum Books for Young Readers
Published by Simon & Schuster
KIDS.SimonandSchuster.com
EBOOK EDITIONS ALSO AVAILABLE